Contents

IN ENVY COUNTRY

THE RICHARD SULLIVAN PRIZE IN SHORT FICTION

Editors
William O'Rourke and Valerie Sayers

JOAN FRANK

IN ENVY COUNTRY

Stories

East Baton Rouge Parish Library
Baton Rouge, Louisiana

Published by the University of Notre Dame Press
Notre Dame, Indiana 46556
www.undpress.nd.edu
All Rights Reserved

Manufactured in the United States of America

Library of Congress Cataloging-in-Publication Data
Frank, Joan.
In envy country : stories / Joan Frank.
p.   cm. — (The Richard Sullivan Prize in short fiction)
ISBN-13: 978-0-268-02888-6 (pbk. : alk. paper)
ISBN-10: 0-268-02888-5 (pbk. : alk. paper)
1. Man-woman relationships—Fiction.   I. Title.
PS3606.R38I52   2009
813'.6—dc22

2009035056

For Ianthe Brautigan

ALSO BY JOAN FRANK

The Great Far Away

Miss Kansas City

Boys Keep Being Born

Acknowledgments

I am grateful to the editors of the following journals, in which these stories first appeared:

"In Envy Country" in *The Baltimore Review*; "A Note on the Type" in the *Chautauqua Literary Journal*; "Picaro" in *Drunken Boat*; "Rearview" in the *GSU Review*; "Sandy Candy" in the *Notre Dame Review*; "Savoir Faire, Savoir Vivre" in *Zone 3*; "The Sun on the Ganges" in the *Seattle Review*; "A Thing That Happens" in *Emrys Journal*.

"Betting on Men," © 2005 by the Antioch Review, Inc., first appeared in the *Antioch Review*, vol. 63, no. 4. Reprinted by permission of the Editors.

———

Heartfelt thanks to these individuals:

Ianthe Brautigan and Bob Duxbury—

the Carabetta, Havens, and Kuehne families—

A NOTE ON THE TYPE

Rochelle appeared at the office one day looking young and somewhat frightened, walking with tentative steps on the arm of her husband, who soon broke away like a discreet booster rocket and disappeared down a stairwell door, leaving her to walk forward alone, more abashed, to meet the rest of us. She was to interview for an accounting position.

My boss, the former kitchenware magnate Gerald Riding, led the way, stepping forward in that strange, tentative toe-walk—it made him look like he was trying to sneak up on something, or as if he might change his mind at any moment and race away. Gerald had finally fired his longtime accountant. What had driven Gerald past his limit was her handwriting, which was not just indecipherable but weirdly ugly. Even a line of it gave the observer an immediate sense of imminent, hideous chaos. Gerald Riding was a tolerant man, himself eccentric—but among his extreme habits was a strict demand for neatness, brevity, coherence. Sometimes Gerald thought he should have been a lawyer. He liked the word "remedy." Old Sarah was asked to turn the business records back over to us.

And Rochelle Remington Banks was hired, straight from her interview in response to the ad Gerald placed. She looked, as I say, young. Pale and timid and countrified, a far different image from that which would replace it in time. Her hair was a wild thatch, I remember; her clothes frowsy and earnest, like the skirts and blouses fading in windows of small-town shops. Her eyes were Betty Boop's: huge and black. Eyes eager to persuade you of their natural sympathy without revealing the least trace of a thinking agency behind them. Those big wet black eyes managed, while taking in great gulps of information, to convey not one fleck of autonomous thought or opinion.

Eyes that waited, rapt.

Rochelle's behavior made the same warrant of emptyvesselhood as did her eyes and even her voice, a piping singsong. She presented herself in those first weeks with self-conscious erectness, a debutante balancing a book on her head— such eager, open *disponibilité* it couldn't help slightly alarm us. For it didn't take long to see that whatever the context, however breathless the words and reverent the posture, Rochelle wanted something.

At first it was information. Sources. Resources. Later it was favors. Might you be kind enough to mail this. Could you phone that, arrange the other. At first I only thought her terrified of making a misstep—that her Sunday school manners, so theatrically inflected, were part of the natural caution at any job's beginning. Jobs fell apart so amusingly later—that was the joke of it. People slouched and slurred and kicked things around after dwelling years together in the same rooms, as if married too long. But beginnings were routinely stiff with performance anxiety, brittle with shiny representations straight off the resumé. *Reliable. Self-starter. Multi-tasking.*

I worked in the bullpen, as we called it: the reception desk for Gerald's printing firm. My desk was positioned smack in front of the elevator, so that the elevator doors opened like theater curtains on a passenger who'd find himself facing an audience of one: me. The joke went that any discontented client or random lunatic might step through those sliding doors one day brandishing an automatic weapon, unloading on whoever was first in view. One old spy movie began exactly this way, and sometimes I did worry about it. *Take this for your typos, you clowns. And this for your rush charge!*

My chores were clerical, comical in retrospect—to include simply letting people in and out of Gerald's building. Yes, the entire building. Lord knew how many millions the old edifice was worth in that upscale section of the city—a zone where successful film stars and rock singers bought mansions, even if they never bothered to live there. Gerald had dipped into his Ridingware dividends to renovate the structure. Amazing, what money could achieve. Once a grimy gray parking garage, now painted and rewired and clean—from the street Gerald's building resembled a snowy, three-layered wedding cake replete with frosting ribbons and chevrons. A television screen on my desk showed me clients approaching the front entrance. When they pressed the downstairs bell an electronic *dingdong* sounded at my station. I'd push the little black button that unlocked the entrance doors—several times in rapid succession, so people below could hear the clicking and realize they should push through. All day long that *dingdong* assailed me, and all day I watched visitors struggling to manage the logic. I came to feel like part of some whimsical social science experiment.

In fact this was not far from true. Gerald enjoyed the doorbell apparatus, having rigged it himself. He had a taste for odd experiments; gathering human beings into unlikely combinations was only one facet of that taste, in perfect calm equivalence with a host of odd others. Gerald had so many oddnesses no one thought twice about them, except as an extension of who he was. He insisted only clear glass plates and cups and bowls be kept in the office kitchen. Any coffee grounds that scattered sent him into a frenzy—we had to blot up each infinitesimal grain. Gerald hauled his daily materials—binders, papers, books, computer parts, a ratty blue sweater—to the office every day in a cardboard box, lugged with both hands as he walked his toe-walk. And yes, he liked to collect people and set them upon each other—but like splashed colors of paint, or instruments for some loony orchestra. Once he'd introduced people he tiptoed away.

His energy bewildered us. A man of sixty, he couldn't have slept more than a few hours a night. At day's end people half his age would be wilted and aching to go home, but Gerald—though the indentations beneath his eyes ran bluegreen—would eat an egg salad sandwich and make a cup of black tea, and stay on into the night. He could be glimpsed through the window at dusk from the street below, sitting at a computer under the second-story's fluorescent ceilings, his scalp glowing pink where his hair was parted. Gerald received income from his shares of the cookware empire which still bore his name, a production imported by plucky immigrants whose business, right from the start, seemed to enjoy sunny popularity no matter what the national economy was doing. Ridingware expanded during the sixties to include dining settings, a kind of American *faience*, modernized in due course to be ovenproof and then microwave-proof, priced to appeal across a broad demographic. With this money, Gerald—who gave not one damn for cooking or dining tools, having less use for them than a badger might—turned to what he'd always loved: printing. Words. Type on paper. The names of the typefaces stirred him: Goudy, Helvetica, Electra, Caledonia, Metro. The names made him think of futuristic cities, or planets in a comic-book galaxy. He would sit in the city library for hours leafing through the back pages of old novels for the lovely final paragraph, "A Note on the Type," its little sketch of historical eras and period styles, its thumbnail biography of the designer, the lore of peculiar difficulties . . . *a practicing type founder in Leipzig who, despite illness and loss, was able to create two more original faces . . .*

The wily variousness of each letter, even as it conformed to the visual elements of its alphabet family, drew Gerald as if to an elegant mathematical proof. It must have soothed his long-ing for a controllable order that expressed, nonetheless, real beauty. We sometimes wondered why Gerald had not opted for a career in calligraphy. I decided his inventor's mind craved the purity of exactitude. Words were still needed—but with computers you could *pour* words, never spilling a drop. He kept several big books of type fonts on his desk, and carried sev-eral more around in his cardboard box. Though our business advertised as print-on-demand, and though it was true we mostly churned out throwaway flyers and business cards and posters stapled to telephone poles—what Gerald loved was de-signing handbills for civic events, like the renaming of a street, or the city opera's annual fundraiser. Concert programs. Con-sulate cocktails. Broadsides for dance recitals, eco-festivals, po-etry readings.

Those jobs made Gerald happy. And when Gerald was happy we could all let down a notch, and be cautiously happy ourselves. Office atmosphere turned on Gerald's mood. When Gerald was angry he went cold and abrupt, and his features took on a pig-faced harshness. Gerald's money made him supreme in that queer, private kingdom. You sometimes hated him, but guiltily, because he'd saved you. Plucked you from the daily floodtide of the lost and lonely—a tide still visible out the office windows, lapping the building's edges in the street below— people slumping along, limp and soggy and faded among the discarded labels and candy-wrappers. Yes, he'd found me among them. A vague, melancholic art student on scholarship; short-tempered, leary, with no living family and no real prospects. Whenever I'd walked past Gerald's building on Hyperion Street I'd notice his firm's posters pasted up on the glass front doors. Someone in typography class told me Gerald was a typeface freak. I walked into his building one day and petitioned Gerald for work like a foundling. When he learned I could type fast and spell well, he hired me on the spot. The entire staff was com-posed of other versions of me. Two impoverished single moth-ers, a drug casualty, an aspiring actress. All single women. All needful. All eager to please.

But our staff's collective memory of Gerald's rescue had dissolved over time, as memory will, giving way to a notion of entitlement. We imagined we owned the jobs he'd kindly dreamed up for us, here in this pretend-business that never made money but served as Gerald's hobby. Gerald paid everything: salaries and supplies and property taxes, even medical expenses. Every week he bought lunch for staff meetings wherein we'd "clarify our direction." People bullied each other, gossiped and fumed. We played at business like kids playing house.

The irony was, Gerald took the printing as seriously as if it gave him his livelihood. He came from great wealth—a county back east was named for his family—and he had never been formally employed in his life, except to attend a tearfully boring Ridingware board meeting in Manhattan once a year. So we would clench up in those bleak moments when he barked at us, his features tightening piggily—and I'd wonder silently, sullenly, *when did you ever have a real job.*

Ah, but Gerald liked women.

Surrounded himself with them. And Rochelle was pretty. Not remarkably so, but her youth and Betty Boop eyes, her pleasantly slender body, gave her a capable, winsome aspect. In fairness, women were easier for Gerald to be among. Men would have scorned him, or been baffled by him. We hirelings formed a protective harem, no denying it, most of us in our early thirties then. At the time we found the harem idea amusing—one of a multitude of glib images to try on, like costumes. We took turns teasing Gerald when we knew he was in a mood for it, laughing and squeezing his arm, a ragtag of spirited colts.

Gerald himself looked like a turn-of-the-century portrait, missing only the bowler balanced on a proffered elbow. His hair was pepper-colored, parted on one side and pasted down with a damp comb. His body was queerly undeveloped, never subject to athletic exertions of any kind. His shoulders were a little boy's—narrow and sloping. In fact Gerald was the shape of an oversized toddler, including a slight potbelly, which after a while I came to believe was the place he put his longing.

Gerald married an anxious young Russian woman he'd met in college. Ludmilla was big-boned with warm, smooth skin—an ad for facial soap—and she, too, came from wealthy importers. But her manner was tentative and importuning, often ending her sentences with a little self-deprecating half-laugh, *eh-heh*. She nonetheless bore Gerald two sturdy daughters, each stamped with a cheerful combination of both parents' features like limited-edition coins. Gerald seemed fond of his family, but at the same time it was clear that family duty chafed and plagued him—slung him with that many more dreary chores, and fewer defensible escapes. How often I answered distressed, fluttery phone calls from Ludmilla—*Oh hi Merin eh-heh, is Gerald there eh heh?*—when she frantically needed him to show up at this place or that. Sometimes I thought Gerald's marrying must have solved a two-pronged problem: it softened his sharp loneliness, but it also veiled his burgeoning strangeness. Thus, he bore the baggage of *pater*hood as stoically as he could. Anyone could see that Gerald would always rather be left alone—except, perhaps, for a bit of female admiration.

The more familiar we were, the better. He'd think of things to say to egg us on, exaggerating the situation we'd named just to hear us howl. It wasn't for titillation: Gerald stood so far outside the living, so apart from any conventional idea of belonging to the regular skirmishes of survival, that people who actually appeared to be grappling with life, cursing and wiping off sweat—these were the real curiosity to him. His own life had been so thickly cushioned—doting aunts and sisters, and always, always, the money—that he could never, as one observer suggested, "slam a door." Gerald was a *voyeur* ogling the phenomenon of mortal engagement.

Rochelle started small.

It was a matter at first of little favors. Finding files for her, or phone numbers. Then it became a series of perky requests. Rochelle sought those comforting services that one needs straightaway in a city: drycleaner, dentist, health food store. A good happy-hour bar, a good Mexican diner. The list blossomed—dance clubs, travel agents, extension classes, gynecologists—and didn't take long to grow braver: used BMWs, discount wine imports, psychiatrists, apartments to let. (Gerald wound up renting her a property of his own, at princely discount.) In each case Rochelle would approach her target with that unmistakable posture—buoyant, erect and sparkly, an adoring child bursting with a delicious secret. The trick of her manner was to flatter her mark, whipping this spell into a sweet foamy froth, installing a kind of fond delirium before the recipient had time to brace for what came next. Rochelle's eyes and face brimmed with admiring delight: *O wonderful one! You radiant spectacle you, you ice cream sundae you.* Her voice all but squealed, coy and Boop-a-doopy, and the target would be temporarily blinded by the sudden atmospheric dazzle while Rochelle tiptoed closer: a favorite daughter approaching her indulgent daddy.

I remember a day I wore a jacket she fancied. It was old brown leather, oversized, from the secondhand store. I'd no idea she fancied it, nor had she in fact—when all at once she burst from her office. She had to race down the street. It was chilly out there. Quick, Merin: loan me your jacket? I tossed it to her just before the elevator doors closed. When they reopened she stepped forth wearing the jacket in her debutante position: intent, smiling. At me.

Merrrrin? Her voice glided upward. Her eyes shone.

I have a proposition for you.

This uttered with twinkling portent.

If I pay for its next cleaning, why don't we *share* this jacket! She spoke the word *share* in a delectable rush, as if Christmas were about to fall through the ceiling on my head. Rochelle wanted to be anointed, that minute, as half-owner of my leather jacket. Why? Because what Rochelle desired, she absolutely believed she deserved. Like the notorious French king who had shrugged, on being asked his motive for some crazy edict, *car tel est mon beau plaisir.* Because such is my royal pleasure.

In the next year, Rochelle had a baby and divorced her husband. Stanley Banks was a tall, homely fellow who'd become a sales executive for a telecommunications franchise. He drove a white convertible and began dating again at once. A vain, irritable man whom no one at the office cared for, Stanley was never missed.

Meantime, Rochelle commenced a friendship with Ludmilla Riding. Little gestures at first. Offers to run errands. Lunches. Shopping. Soon the two were confessing their life's dreams over glasses of merlot, and Rochelle had elicited Ludmilla's most cherished theories of childrearing and world harmony.

I remember the day Rochelle emerged from the elevator in her best posture, and with a flourish plonked a basket on the countertop fronting my bullpen. Women on staff came running from every direction while I stood up and gazed in: a tiny pink creature with Rochelle's pug nose wrapped papoose-tight in blankets, nested in her Moses-like carrier of woven reeds. Windowlight from the street played over the pink baby, who stirred and grimaced. Rochelle stood by, glowing with authorship as the women made the noises women make when they flock to view a new infant—but Gerald was nowhere to be seen. Where is Gerald?, someone finally thought to ask. I found him a room away, crouched at his terminal as if in a dugout trench during mortar fire. Gerald, c'mon, I urged him: Rochelle's baby is here! He edged toward the infant, glanced, nodded nervously as we commanded he admire the blinking yawning Delia, her squinched face and fine fuzz of blonde down.

That's very nice, he said at last, rocking slightly from heel to toe. Very nice.

Then he darted away.

Rochelle tried bringing the baby to work a few more times, perching the basket at her feet next to her desk, but Gerald's discomfort was plain. Soon she had arranged to give the baby during the day into the care of Ludmilla's Salvadoran housekeeper,

Alma. What was another little baby to Alma, who capably handled her own three small children, the Ridings' two girls, and housecleaning into the bargain? Once again the cost to Rochelle was nil. Likely Gerald and his wife viewed his new young accountant to be caught in a poignant jam. She was now divorced, working fulltime, and deserving—as Ludmilla reminded her husband, hands on hips—of the same consideration he'd want for his own wife and children, was she not?

After a brief trial period Rochelle went to Gerald to assure him it was absolutely necessary she have an assistant to handle monthly payroll, taxes, and all regular payables and receivables. Gerald agreed at once, and a shy Swedish grandmother with short white hair came to perform these tasks three days each week. Rochelle's child was being minded all day, and her main work was delegated. What did that leave Rochelle to do?

It left her free.

Free to arrange things. Rochelle commandeered her private office phone. Bikini waxes, psychic readings, makeovers. Scuba lessons. Spanish lessons. Acting lessons. Singing lessons. Yoga. Home and garden shows. Car shows. Rebirthing sessions. Deep tissue massage. We grew accustomed to seeing Rochelle trip in and out of the office all the business day, tossing a quick, joyful word to me about her official (wink) whereabouts for the next few hours. Slipping into the elevator and taking her debutante position—shoulders back, brimming with anticipation—the elevator doors slid together over her image like the closing segue of a movie segment.

At these gay farewells I always nodded, relieved to be rid of her. By then none of us was any longer much fooled—at least, none of us on Gerald's staff—by the flung-glitter of Rochelle's act. Where Rochelle was, unease crept in. A funny taste filtered through your awareness in her wake, like after you drank milk that had turned.

But it was too late for Gerald, trussed now by so many interlocked strips and layers it would be like peeling off skin to undo. Ludmilla had felt very pleased and excited when she persuaded Rochelle that toddling Delia should attend the same private school (feeder preschool and kindergarten) as did the Riding girls. Naturally Gerald, who happened to be co-founder of that exclusive school, would authorize the scholarship for the struggling single mother. Soon Rochelle and toddler Delia were asked to accompany the Riding family on holiday retreats to the Riding country home, a jutting wooden structure in the mountains just a stone's skip from the sapphire-colored lake. Alma was by then also cleaning Rochelle's apartment, located a few convenient blocks from the Riding mansion. Rochelle and Ludmilla began setting off together to hear lectures by visiting spiritual leaders—Ludmilla felt deep stirrings of connection to specialists in past-lives, to channelers of the wise ancients. Rochelle acted on Ludmilla's behalf during these outings, as scout and escort. She navigated them through lobbies, steering Ludmilla's arm, negotiating tickets and directions and exits, waiting patiently for Ludmilla at restroom doors, ordering for them in noisy restaurants. Their children now played together after school every day like siblings. Rochelle had entered the family.

At the same time, she never lost sight of Gerald.

The two met in late morning with the office door closed. Together they reviewed the personal entreaties that poured in for Gerald, and Gerald would dictate his responses. People the world over knew of the eccentric heir to the Ridingware fortune, and the schemes begging his funding arrived daily, various as snowflakes. This one proposed selling pieces of the recently decimated Berlin Wall. That one sought to scan satellite-video relays. Save the Earth. Save the Whales. Save the Organic Farmer. Rochelle came to assume an air that announced her representation—her protection—of Gerald Riding. She became, in effect, his agent. She accompanied him to ceremonies, even spoke for him. Rochelle took the podium with the same book-balancing posture, but now with stricter authority. She would glance at her notes as she spoke, raising her head periodically to meet the eyes of people around the room, just as she'd been coached by her private, Gerald-paid, tutor. Rochelle gazed with calm pride at her listeners, with all the warm dignity the occasion could want.

By this stage, Rochelle sported a trendy haircut and vivid clothing. Tasty little suits, higher heels, *chic* boots and trenchcoats, bags of rich leather, makeup that emphasized those lustrous, black eyes. She took facials and mudbaths, manicures, pedicures, papaya-enzyme purges. She had colonics, aura-manipulations, electrolysis. She ordered regular shipments of expensive vitamin supplements. An ion-cleanser, which resembled an oblong car radiator, buzzed away in her office. I never heard Rochelle ask the price of anything. I never learned what Gerald paid her. I tried not to think about it.

For myself? I was an art student, remember. I rented a studio out by the park, near an avenue from which, if you gazed to where it met the horizon, you could see a thumbnail-tip of blue ocean. My little place was a handy block from the main streetcar line. I thought of it as a second-floor shoebox, with holes cut in the lid. Stashed my charcoals and drawings there, and when I wasn't brooding over these spent many hours on the floor nearest the wall heater, legs propped straight up against it, reading or watching television with a glass of wine. From time to time the office or one of its clients threw a party, and out of boredom and loneliness and some infernal spark of annoying hope, I'd force myself to shower and change and catch the streetcar to these evenings.

I remember one New Year's Eve bash at the famous old Italian restaurant, for which we printed menus. The dimmed light of the wharfside bar made its picture-window views mysteriously luminous—graygreen sea at dusk, ferries motoring along strung with lights—while inside, a mist of champagne-filled glasses shimmered against the candlelit satin of women's cocktail sheaths. Ludmilla was elsewhere that night, helping with one of the children's holiday pageants. Restaurant workers danced and joked with guests; noise and recklessness ruled—that unique, sad abandon of another year marked done.

In the roar of the midnight countdown I glimpsed Rochelle, in a brilliant red silk dress, appear suddenly as an apparition before Gerald, throw her arms around his neck and kiss him. The dress was sleeveless and diaphanous; a length of it flowed back over her shoulders. Her upper arms were white and full. Womanly ripeness swirled so easily with daughterly intimacy, there was no telling where either began or ended. Streamers and confetti were raining, hand-blown horns and noisemakers honked and bleated, and someone near the light switches flicked them rapidly off and on to make the soft bulbs blink in a strobe effect.

I love you, Gerald, Rochelle's mouth shaped the words in the din as she held his face in her hands. (I could read the words easily enough, though it was impossible to hear.) Her eyes sought his teasingly, endearingly half-lidded, the way a poodle-owner might speak to her beloved pet.

Everyone by then was well-dosed with champagne.

Gerald blinked at her as though a trance had been interrupted: pleased, curious, a kid becoming aware he'd just tasted something good. He wore his same old blue sweater. Abruptly, his eyes crinkled merrily. *I love you, too, Rochelle,* his mouth shaped the words back to her. But as I watched I saw that Gerald was not breathing hard; not heavy-eyed. Not thickened and slowed with desire. Instead, he was cheerful. Imitative. Game. A happy parakeet mimicking human speech, or a space alien learning traffic signals. That was when I began to comprehend Gerald's confused innocence. Of course he had his fantasies, but they were desperately mixed up with a kind of permanent wonder at the gestures of adult life. Though he had sired children, his inmost sensibility remained a child's. Gerald would do his best to ape the apparent currency of the culture at hand. If custom dictated one kissed and declared love at midnight New Year's Eve, why, he'd do as the aboriginals did.

Soon enough, Rochelle began dating.

Exploring the opportunities, she called it. Taking initiative. She placed ads for her ideal mate in the city's weeklies and on internet bulletin boards. Her calendar must have been busier than a president's. I watched her come and go. If you had set up a camera in front of my desk and filmed her various forays, then fast-forwarded the film, it would have looked like a frantic old silent movie: Rochelle ratcheting in and out of the elevator a thousand times, each time pausing a millisecond to make elaborate gestures, mouth working, openshut openshut, giving careful, explicit instructions to me.

An assortment of males began to appear. They'd walk out of the elevator toward me—casually, because to show eagerness was bad form. They'd lean on my countertop.

Hi. Rochelle here?

Just a minute, please. I'd buzz Rochelle and she'd promise to appear in a moment. Then the boy would wander around, staring at some of Gerald's posters on the walls. Cool, he'd sometimes remark politely. Unfortunately Gerald's posters were all the same. Since he craved minimalism and symmetry, all his printed announcements took the shape, from a distance, of a Rorschach inkblot test or a multi-tiered candy dish. And despite his access to every typeface on earth, he always used the same font. Garamond.

The boy would soon wander back to me and lean against the front of my bullpen. I had to make small talk. So. What do you do?

One was a stockbroker. Another, a small-plane pilot. A real estate sales guy. An ad agency guy with a wee ponytail. A sous-chef. An actor. One ran a sensitivity-training retreat in Carmel. They were prospectors, just like the ones who'd staked claims in Colorado or the Sierras, or the young soldiers waltzing young women around in old Russian novels. Perhaps each of us only amounts to some form of this in the end: perhaps it is only a matter of degree. Rochelle would return to the office after each tryst to tell about them. A picnic at Land's End. Dancing at the Stardust Lounge. At first the rest of us on staff listened like chorines in a Broadway musical. We tried to track each episode and to cheer for whomever it was Rochelle seemed to want. (The real estate guy owned a property on a wealthy island in the bay. Rochelle wanted to share the estate with him, the way she'd offered to share my jacket. He stopped phoning.) Soon we wearied of listening. Her reports began to wane. I knew Rochelle was growing impatient. A new tack was needed, a new target. It wasn't long before she'd crafted her answer.

The city at hand wasn't bearing fruit? Travel out of it.

Rochelle chose Greece. The island of Paros. Someone told her it was still unspoiled—one of those secret destinations of the avant garde, Rochelle confided to me in lilting, jubilant tones. She had no difficulty persuading Gerald that her journey would be good for everyone and everything. It made me wince later to consider that conversation. Rochelle would never describe it. But she did insist, after everything else had happened—after all of it was over—on telling me the rest.

What she did not supply, I could certainly envision.

Rochelle flew to Athens, which looked like one vast, seedy miracle-mile, crumbling sheds and shacks and tire shops, scraps and auto parts, garbage and noise. Athens frightened her with its beggars and wizened grifters, its miles of dust and chaos. It was August, chokingly hot. She found a bus to the harbor, paid her ticket for a big interisland ferry to Paros. Gulls cried and wheeled, the late afternoon sun grainy through a haze of seasalt, diesel fumes, dust. From the dock the ship loomed like a skyscraper, boarding cars, trucks, huge cargo-containers, lines of people streaming like ants into its cavernous hold. She feared for the vessel's floatability, but was glad to finally watch the hot brown mainland recede, with a single visible brooch in its filthy bosom—the Parthenon, small and mute and bone-white, shrinking as the distance opened between her ship and the city, wind riffling the gray water. As darkness came she slept in her passenger chair; others on the carpeted floor, others on the wide-slatted deck while the cement craft motored its course.

Dimitri Diamantis was waiting with the others as the giant vessel hefted into the port at Parikia. You didn't notice anyone standing there until you'd made your way down the steep gangplank with the dozens of other backpackers. A scraggly lineup of indifferent faces. A few old women in kerchiefs. Men with tight cotton shirts and pants. Boys racing in circles. Dust and smells of bundled fruit, frying meat, and the salt-sea surging around the ship, falling over itself at the edge of land in weak blips.

He looks like an actor, was Rochelle's first thought. Soft brown hair, curling, slicked back on the sides. Dense dark brows permanently bunched over squinting eyes. His skin wasn't good but it was strangely provocative, rough. He stood quietly, ignoring the clamor on all sides—as if not deigning to squander a moment's awareness on it.

Mitso—she soon took up the local diminutive—was one of those types who could have come from anywhere, could have been Italian, Welsh, Israeli. The thing he clearly wasn't was American. A traveler abroad soon recognizes American DNA— that fleshy insouciance feeding into lips and hair, the meaty way the body sheaths its bones. There was the quiet absence in Mitso of an American's raw assumption of space. Instead, the young man was made of something more compressed, not as well nourished. The volatile Other. The mystery ride. So alike, on blurry face of it—humanoid, biped, westernized—yet so utterly not.

You need hotel. He asked it—stated it—as if someone else had said it, and he'd casually overheard.

Rochelle did, in fact.

You come my hotel. Big, clean, very beautiful. On beach. Beautiful white beach.

Again, he recited these facts as if patient, but bored. Smells of frying potatoes drifted from the harbor. Around them flowed people speaking many languages, animals, crates and big coarse burlap bags, a squawking, scurrying throng. After establishing the hotel's reasonable price, Rochelle accepted. It was a bright, hot morning, the sunlight bouncing blindingly off sea and white sand. Mitso had a hotel bus; she was very tired; other tired backpackers had accepted. If it proved a scam she'd already be stationed in town in the middle of day, on the main road by the glittering water.

Mitso made it easy for Rochelle.

He was at her side at breakfast, which she took on the outdoors deck, consisting of a bowl of coffee lightened with milk, bread with butter (curiously, always slightly rancid) and honey. His family—grandparents, mother, younger brother—owned the little beachside hotel, living behind and above it in a series of small apartments—and Mitso had acted some years now as its chief mascot, advocate, and procurer. Mitso told Rochelle he was a law student at the university in Athens; he was just now having his summer holiday. He meant to practice in Athens, he said. Corporate law, he told her. In two years, when he passed the bar.

In the foreground he cut a handsome, lonely figure.

He would appear from the lobby doors on the patio where she sat alone at one of the little white plastic tables, drinking her bowl of milky Nescafé. When he emerged he'd typically look pale and badly used; God knew how many Santé cigarettes and *ouzos* had coursed through him. He was thin, wore clinging dark pants and almost transparent white cotton shirts open to the navel. Against his smooth chest rested a gold chain at whose vortex dangled an old-fashioned crucifix. Rochelle knew he had seen her sitting there, but instead of coming directly to her he would cross to the railing enclosure and look out to sea. Warm ozone haze already draped the shimmering blue air, which still breathed morning sweetness: the light more like mist, topaz blue, reverberant from above and below. The mountains, Rochelle noted, were like the desert mountains she'd driven through with Stan in Arizona, big benign curves, arid and scrubby brown, but here they were set on an island in the sea. They looked like pictures from children's Bible stories. Pigeons and gulls strutted boldly around the white plastic table legs, turning their heads to the side, eyeing the cement floor for crumbs. Mitso would light a cigarette and squint out at the misty blue light. His face always seemed rumpled and pained with some profound complication. Rochelle could never suppress the reflex that his *dolor* was something she should address—something it was in her power to cure.

Finally he would float forward as if by chance, to speak with her. Have you seen the island, all around, he murmured the first time. No, she hadn't yet ventured beyond the beachfront strip where she'd encamped the day the Athens ship brought her. If you like I show you, he said, his brown eyes regarding her as if from beneath cool rippling pools. Rochelle believed she would like that. She climbed onto Mitso's *mihanaki* behind him while he held it upright for her, snugged her arms around his lean waist—he smelled like cigarettes and sugar— and off they sped spewing smelly exhaust, making a sound like an angry tree-saw. They zoomed past young men walking, past skinny dogs and sunburnt tourists. They saw the weatherworn houses tucked in the wild brush on dry, remote terraces. They stopped to buy her a straw hat against the merciless sun. They stood at cliff's edge to regard the dim outlines of the island Antiparos, and the *ploio*, the boats on the shining afternoon water. They tramped up a steep dirt path to a restaurant where Mitso knew the owner, and in the blessed cool of the dark canteen they drank frappés of heavily sweetened coffee, while through the open door swallows flittered and chuckled in the branches of the olive trees.

Rochelle wrote postcards to Gerald and Ludmilla praising the beauty of the island, but she did not mention Mitso. How far her old existence—its shoulder pads and face-care systems, its time-management urgencies—seemed from the lazy warmth of this seaside town! How much more sense the pace of Mitso's world made! Rochelle thought she should by rights be able to transplant her life here: to this sunbleached hotel across the street from the turquoise ocean, with nothing more to do each day than tote her paperback and bottled water to the beach, wander back at night for some dinner; later walk into town to the blaring disco bars with Mitso—while he was home on breaks from school, of course. Her mind cupped protecting hands around the image: vibrant American wife to handsome young Greek lawyer. She'd heard that tony neighborhoods were to be found outside Athens, some with real villas, surrounded by pines. Or perhaps she and Mitso could make their home right here on Paros—she'd glimpsed the ranch-style houses popping up in its hills. Mitso could commute to Athens by *vapori*. Of course, Rochelle missed Delia. She phoned the girl every two days; Delia was playing contentedly with the Riding sisters in their nursery. They had visited the circus, she informed her mother. Rochelle was thinking quickly, flitting and light, like a bat feeling out the parameters of a room. Delia could live here most of the year with herself and Mitso: Stanley could have her on holidays. If there were no English-language schools Rochelle could hire a bilingual tutor—a tutor for herself and for Delia. Mitso would adore the child. The Diamantis family would take the blonde toddler to its heart. Teach her the folkways. Care for her while Rochelle and Mitso made getaways to other islands, to Paris or London or Madrid. Rochelle woke to these visions each morning, stretching dreamily inside her clean, starchy sheets. If she bore down on the notion with all her ferocious will, something would happen.

Something had to.

After a week's time, Mitso asked her to meet his family. Rochelle's chest squeezed.

But I speak no Greek, she demurred, taking his hands. They'll think I'm just another dumb tourist.

Mitso shook his head, smiling sadly. You very important, very beautiful, he said. I want they see. He pressed his lips to the knuckles of both her hands, his eyes never leaving hers.

Rochelle believed she'd made a hit with the Diamantis clan. A bit dazed, she'd sat down beside Mitso at an oilcloth-covered table upstairs and nodded and smiled with painful brightness as his extended kin roared all around her, arguing and joking in Greek, passing delicacies—lamb stew, potatoes in garlic and oil, hunks of tough bread, salad of tomatoes and cucumbers, goat cheese, yogurt with honey. They pointed at her with their sodas and lemonade and retsina; they smacked Mitso on the shoulder, talking and laughing raucously. "*Fili*," they grinned at him. When they laughed their mouths opened widely and Rochelle could see their teeth, yellow and snaggled and cracked, some of them gold, some missing completely. Mitso did not share their hilarity, nodding or shrugging tightly as he ate. He translated for her only when Rochelle prodded him.

They say you very smart, very beautiful, he said. Then: They want you tell them about California, he added with dark embarrassment.

Rochelle dutifully described the state's northern half, its deep woods, mountains and beaches, orchards and vegetable farms. Mitso translated in rapid, somewhat irritated fashion. Rochelle guessed he felt possessive of her, and this touched her. The family listened: black-skirted *yia yia* with her fierce brows, *pappou* listlessly agreeable in his trousers and sweat-dampened shirt, bustling aproned mother and skinny little brother and who knew how many "cousins," their eyes darting, mutely flickering with a light that Rochelle couldn't identify. But she felt sure she'd made an impression, insisting that Mitso repeat to them how much she admired the island, their food and hospitality. As soon as he could, Mitso excused the two of them and asked her to walk with him on the beach, under the moon. They stepped around rocks in the sand. Mitso turned to her mid-step, and told her he loved her.

Rochelle went back to Paros to see Mitso once more, after the difficulties had begun. None of us knew, just then, what was wrong.

We only knew that not long after her first visit to Greece Rochelle began arriving to work at the office pale and distraught. It was late autumn by then. The air had sharpened, leaves of trees along the walks turning pewter, light over the city diffuse and fragile. At the time we did not question her, and she did not volunteer anything. We all went about our normal duties and tried to reincorporate Rochelle into the slangy rhythms of office gossip. She smiled, listened wanly, and soon withdrew to her desk. Something about her was altered, but none of us could pinpoint it.

She had first arrived back from her vacation tanned and euphoric. We knew she had met someone called Dimitri in the Greek islands, about whom she'd initially raved—I'd spotted several calls to Parikia on the company telephone bill—but she'd soon gone silent on the subject. I never saw her speaking directly to Gerald during that period, though sometimes when the door to Gerald's office was closed I knew both were inside. I could hear their voices, low and urgent, though I couldn't make out the words. At about the same time I noticed Gerald's moods becoming shorter, his mouth pursed in that sour line we'd learned to dread. He didn't respond to our teasing, nor initiate any of his little mischiefs. He sat all day at his computer fussing with type—trying to perfect the curve on a serif in blocky blown-up pixels, never pleased with the scaled-down result. Some days he didn't appear at all. My co-workers, sensing a bad patch, moved softly. Even the front-entrance *dingdong* seemed mournful and plaintive.

Outside, the streets glistened silver with winter rains.

Rochelle's chummy dates with Ludmilla lapsed. She tended to go straight home after picking up Delia, and during the business day I no longer watched her flash in and out of the elevator, taking her debutante position with its pert, expectant glow. Instead as the doors closed upon her I saw a different Rochelle, a Rochelle Picasso might have painted: broad cheekbones at disjointed angles, hair lifting in cockeyed lumps, skin porous and custard-hued, gaze glassy—staring at something invisible, and far away.

I learned long afterward that Rochelle had returned to Paros the second time on a mission. She had made a discovery shortly after returning to the American mainland, and she had placed several phone calls. She had conferred with Gerald privately. Then she went back to Parikia to make her most impassioned stand.

She found herself sitting at the edge of the sagging single mattress in Mitso's bare room out behind the hotel, talking to his back. It was broaching winter, and the room was gray and cold. Mitso was wearing a Yale sweatshirt, standing before a clouded mirror propped on a wooden bureau, combing his soft brown hair.

But I am carrying your child, she heard herself pleading. Though she had waited weeks and flown many hours at extreme cost to say it, the actual predicament imbedded in the words—words from daytime television serials—still so astonished her it splintered open in her mind like a dashed bottle as she spoke, filling her throat with shards, making her voice break.

Mitso flicked an exhausted glance sideways at her in the mirror. His brown eyes were dull and hard. You never understand. I am *kamaka*.

He turned to face her, hands braced behind him on the bureau. You know what is *kamakia*?

Rochelle didn't know. *Kamakia*—the singular meant harpoon—were the young men who picked up tourist women in the ports. Many kamakia kept a running tally of their conquests during a season. Tourist women were easier and less expensive than paid prostitutes. And without risk to the family.

The family!

But Mitso, your family liked me!

His upper lip lifted, a brief curl. I told them *fili*. *Friend*, he said.

My family curious, he went on. They like hear you tell California. They want visit California. I too, want visit California! he added fiercely, stabbing his thumb at his own chest.

But the Diamantises had well understood what their eldest son, their hotel's procurer, was about. It was a silently acknowledged axiom that his position gave constant access to attractive female travelers. Rochelle was one in a long line. In any case, the Diamantis grandparents and *mana* and *adelphos* with whom

Rochelle had dined were not the only family Mitso was talking about.

He looked at her. I am married, he muttered, looking away.

Mitso kept a wife and three small children on the island of Syros.

Nikos, Spiros and Irini stayed with his wife's mother, who rented out her own set of pension apartments. It was cheaper. Mitso visited when he felt like it, sent what bits of money he could. Everyone on Paros knew. What was more, Mitso was no law student. He was no student at all. He would take over the hotel operation when his grandparents, and then his mother, died. It was the best he could aspire to.

He looked at Rochelle bitterly. She would have opportunities he could not dream of. And now his escape to them, through her, would be cut off.

You know these things! Why you come back here? Why act like you not know?

If Gerald Riding was detached from human strife, he was the more terrified of getting into the ring with it, of getting bloody. He loved running away, slipping from the room before he could be called on for an opinion. He kept a big sign in the lobby, hung at eye level just by the elevator doors: *Any work produced by this firm is in no way meant to represent the philosophy or beliefs of this firm.* How that sign annoyed me—his skittering dread of taking any kind of stand. Maybe he wanted to avoid the messy, repetitive work of it—of maintaining and defending a stand. Maybe he found it embarrassing. But beneath that, if I am honest, I know Gerald was afraid.

When a week passed after Rochelle's final return from Greece and she had not shown up at work, I recorded the time as sick leave. The Monday she did appear she was paler than ever, but steady. For all I knew, she'd soon be plotting her next wily campaign. She kept to her office all day, as did Gerald; they were not seen together amidst the building's usual noisome Monday traffic.

But they were heard.

I swear I had not meant to eavesdrop that day, while the late afternoon light, delicate as pollen, deepened to translucent teal. I simply found my cold hand unable to place the phone receiver back into its glossy black-plastic pod, after intercoming the office Gerald and Rochelle shared. Gerald had barked at me to hold all calls, and I could hear Rochelle weeping.

What are you saying, what are you saying, I heard her sob.

Placing my free hand tightly over the mouthpiece, I swiveled my chair toward the fading light of the windows and hunched down with the receiver.

Gerald spoke like a machine. The voice of the ticket-spitting device at a parking garage. He kept repeating the same sentence. *You will abide by the conduct code . . . until such time as you decide to leave the business and the family.*

You will abide! Until such time as! Gerald must have written the sentence out and memorized it like a mantra, before he faced her. Was he even looking at her as he spoke?

Rochelle was still crying. But I've not harmed you, Gerald. I'll pay you back. No one knows. I've not brought disgrace—

Each time she tried to speak his voice cut her off, repeating his mantra. A robot voice: the voice he used to rebuff telemarketers. Flat, nasal, pseudo-neutral, no punctuation. A child banging his own ears and chanting, so as not to hear. *Thank you very much I'm not interested. Thank you very much I'm not interested.* Again and again, each time Rochelle tried to engage him. It might have been the sound of rhythmic slapping.

Gerald had been obliged to pay for Rochelle's entire Greek saga, including its culmination, its little murder. He, Gerald Ingersoll Riding, had enabled, willingly or not, what is briskly called in obstetrics-gynecology a *termination*.

The thing inside him that dreaded moral involvement had screamed and writhed. The only way through it was to become someone else. Someone who could wall out such fright forever. Demand fealty to the kingdom, or decree banishment from the kingdom.

That which had been Rochelle's playground became her prison in a stroke.

In theory, of course, Rochelle could have walked out that very hour. And then?

Collect her child from Gerald's mansion; move out of Gerald's apartment that evening? Start again in this city, or another? First and last months' rents? Decent schools for Delia? Childcare? Clothing, food, travel? With what pay, from what job, for what actual work? So deeply had Rochelle burrowed into the Riding family, gorged on its syrupy blood—it seemed impossible to crawl out, to create it all again.

I thought then of a television documentary about the heiress Doris Duke and her domestic entourage—cook, butler, chauffeur, maid. These characters fought viciously, after she died, for pieces of her estate. A Polaroid showed them posed around the aging Duke—her senses steadily draining from her—like demonic family, crouching and ruddy. Her staff had grafted to her like ticks. Part of the organism. Oh, there was no thought of leaving. No universe but the kingdom at hand.

Rochelle kept crying and crying. That's all I heard through the intercom after a while. With excruciating care, I replaced the receiver.

I left the printing office soon thereafter and moved to a tiny north coast town—village, really—to teach art in the little grade school. It feels far away here, wrapped in sea-smelling fog; low horns warning where the shore goes rocky, long grass in the dunes. On the rare occasions when I drive down to the city for supplies, it's like sightseeing from a time machine. I still prowl the car slowly past the wedding-cake building on Hyperion Street, straining my eyes at the second floor. The windows are always empty.

Once, years ago, as if in random answer to my formless wondering, Rochelle Remington phoned me: a question about my address, for a tax form. It was then she told me the events of Greece, and its aftermath.

Her voice was what struck me. Nothing like the stagy warble we used to flinch to hear. All that bursting, witless cheer—entirely gone. I wondered briefly whether she were on something. She told me she still worked for the Ridings. Delia was growing up. Stan had remarried. The printing business was defunct, but everything else, Rochelle declared, was the same. No—she answered quickly—she was seeing no one. There were no plans to change that.

Rochelle's telephone voice that day told me what had changed. Her words edged along some terrible abyss, such as you hear in the voices of scarcely recovered alcoholics or drug addicts. As if an operation had been performed. Scooped out were the debutante's wiles, the flounce and flourish, the gloating, reckless entitlement of *mon beau plaisir*. Replacing all that was the sound of something dazed—trained to venture so far, and no farther. How palpable, how reliable to our landscape is the force of personality! A vitality gone missing, even when wicked, accuses us somehow—of something unspeakable. Against all reason, one almost wished the whole blind over-bright project were restored to her—that self-help world like a shiny board game, with its hyper-earnest tenets, its gleaming appliances, its deadly innocence.

A THING THAT HAPPENS

Sara Bream gathered her breath so that her pillowy twenty-year-old chest, in its soft China-blue sweater, filled to even greater, lovelier loft: she let it out slowly and forcefully. Another evening at which to *present*. Another gathering where she would smile and affirm and help.

She studied her image in the mirror. Smooth, bright skin—some baby fat still at the cheeks. Satin-blonde hair, clear, mirthful blue eyes, an attending sweetness around the mouth. No adult would have guessed fatigue, but tonight she'd much rather have lain under a tree somewhere next to Colin.

Colin was visiting: nephew of her adored Aunt Lily. He was so many things Sara admired: lean, smart, worldly. He worked on a cruise ship—imagine it—all year round, a big fancy liner.

In the bar of its fancy restaurant. He would cook that restaurant's specialty tonight, just for Lily's dinner guests: linguini with red clam sauce. And Sara had in fact already cut to the chase. She had "lain" with Colin. Quaint term!

Oh, but it wasn't like *that*: the young man was not kin to Sara because Lily wasn't Sara's real aunt. Sara's family and Aunt Lil's had lived a few blocks from one another as their children grew up. The families spent so much time together they may as well have moved in together. People had more than once pointed this out, to which both families joked uneasily: they could never afford the mortgage, or they'd fight over the TV remote. Lil was married to Anson Talbot, an affable, hardworking electrical engineer, and they had a young son, Emery. Sara and her parents, Stephen and Claudia, loved the Talbots like blood siblings. Parties were thrown by each clan for each on pretext of the slightest good news: when Sara got her partial scholarship to Oberlin, her Uncle Anson actually found and cooked a whole goose. There was a kind of golden symmetry about the two families— one dark-haired son, one flaxen-haired daughter—the children unusually close to the grown people. When Sara came home on holiday breaks like this one, dinners together happened almost nightly, taking turns between the two houses, with all the two families' friends and neighbors stopping in. Colin was one of a steady stream: the Talbots and the Breams were the sort that had houseguests year-round, often for a month or two at a stretch. But Sara hadn't slept with any, until now.

The minute Sara met Colin, she'd felt herself start to soften in recognizable ways. His manner was easy, his looks delicious, like a mocha cake. And of course he'd already been around the world. But Sara was receiving a first-rate education, thanks to the partial scholarship—and her father's labor. Stephen ran a landscape maintenance company. After years of dogged work, he was established now with a faithful and moneyed clientele; what you called "high-end." He never stinted on his family's needs, but he loved playing the stern captain and dispensing moral bromides. Sara, grateful and sunny, adored her parents. She'd had many frank talks with them about love and sex, goals and destiny—she knew better at this stage than to float mistily toward some notion of romantic endings. She had college to finish, and Colin could not break his contract with the liner. It was good money for him, and his own life kept an unplanned quality that was not practical for her at the moment, though of course it held its temptations. The two young people seemed to come to a quick understanding, without relinquishing admiration for each other. The older people sighed with relief—they would not have to argue Sara out of an early marriage and a move to Wales. But for all their professed liberalism, the older people still felt a bit awkward to know that Sara had had sex with Colin. (She'd told her parents right away: they'd of course told her aunt and uncle.) It was certainly a new day in a new world, the elders thought, blinking.

Tonight, Ruby and Evan were coming over. Sara smiled at her baby-white teeth in the mirror. She loved Ruby and Evan. Ruby was a writer, strong and smart; sort of exotically pretty—the kind of woman Sara thought a Good Model. She was keeping a secret list of them in her journal—women she'd decided made good models of how to be. Who to be. Especially as you got older. The sort who was doing something for herself and standing eye-to-eye with people. Ruby talked so well. Sara always felt a kind of perplexed stirred-up pleasure, listening to her go on about things. But in fact whenever they chatted, it was mainly Ruby who listened to Sara, a kind of mild musing on her face. Sara, who'd grown up nested in loyal praise, fancied Ruby was admiring her. (Ruby brought her special books to read. But when Sara tried these titles, they often struck her as distressingly weird or hard to follow, or so sad she felt she would drown in the heavy porridge of them. Ruby said not to worry if you could not "enter" a book right away, but just to wait a while because eventually an opening would appear. Sara pictured an invisible mushy place that let you pass through a wall, like a famous old creepy television episode.) Sara kept trying to meet Ruby for coffee during school breaks, but Ruby always seemed to have one kind of work or another to go to. And when she, Ruby, apologized for that, there was always a tired sadness about her eyes. Sara thought Ruby acted angry with herself as if she'd committed some early blunder that now resulted in exhaustion—for not having arranged her life the right way, whatever that was. Sometimes Sara noticed Evan teasing Ruby about not having finished college, and then Ruby would send him a hard look and remind him of her lately earned master's degree. Evan always managed to change the subject, laughing. Well, Sara certainly did understand Busy, anyway. Everyone having far too much to do; the whole world gasping, bulging-eyed, clutching its lists, bumping into itself at every corner.

That's why she thought she'd just like to go lie under a tree with Colin and watch the leaves fall, before he had to fly home. It was glorious late autumn, and shocking colors flashed like taunts in the midst of blander shrubs and trees; the fields beyond a mowed, pale green. Sometimes when she and Colin were running errands for her mother, they'd have to pull the car over to gawk: let the deep, wineberry reds and bourbon golds, the opals and buffed dubloons, soak into their eyes. Then Colin would slip his arm around her and turn to her. Warm, cocoa-skinned; even his breath was sweet. *What a smile on that boy.* Sara couldn't help smiling again into the mirror as she touched her lashes with a light mascara. And he was so polite and kind to her family, and to Aunt Lil's. When his lips were beside her ear and his hands in her hair, Colin would murmur a kind of chant, as if he were drunk. "Gorgeous. Gorgeous. Got m'self a beauty queen, didn't I." Though when he said this, it abraded her slightly because it seemed he was talking to himself more than to her; still, it made Sara feel like a rare prize indeed. She would flush tenderly then, as if she were radiating light from all parts of her.

Downstairs Sara helped everywhere she could, as usual. Aunt Lil loved the traditions of each season, and the house was filled with autumn bouquets. She loved a glittering table, and the appropriate ware stood to hand. China, crystal, silver, several bottles of the better wines. A reedy gold-and-red leaf cluster graced the table's center. Ivory-colored candles, fine-weave linen napkins. Emery had scrawled each guest's name on an autumn leaf and placed it beside each plate. Outside, the two black labs woofed excitedly in play with each other, and a few hummingbirds could still be seen through the kitchen window, darting down to drink—their whirring wings a translucent cone—from the tube of sweet red liquid hung out for them.

It was the region's best time.

Sara hummed as she worked. Uncle Anson had a gin-tonic going as he tore fresh spinach, sliced tomatoes, popped the container of oily black Greek olives. Emery was carefully transferring the hot bread from the baking tray to its cloth-lined basket. Aunt Lil whipped cream for the pies. Colin whirled as he readied his garlicky clam sauce and pasta. By the time Evan and Ruby and Claudia and Stephen appeared, spirits had built to typical effervescence, and after the coat-doffing and champagne toasts, people were seated to gaze fondly at one another: champagne assured fondness so reliably.

Don't my parents look handsome, the sweethearts, thought Sara. She pondered the two late-middle-age adults across the table as if they were cute twin eggs she'd long guarded. Stephen had white hair that waved back, and a devilish, grinning-elf face. Claudia, who was a school nurse, had a vague, absorbed attention that soothed people at once; a trusting, dreamy quality about her eyes that repeated in Sara's own. Besides their startling clarity of delicate blue, there was that enormous expectation-of-good in them.

Aunt Lil had a Princess Di face tempered by salt-and-pepper hair in a no-nonsense, brush-back cut. Her eyes were gray-green and kind. Uncle Anson had crew-cut dark hair and a goatee. His cheeks were round as those of the Santas in Coca-Cola ads, and he played host with a burnished air of modest and generous fellowship. Emery, the happy result of the best genes of the two, resembled a ten-year-old Tyrone Power. Sara worried sometimes about the boy's ego in a year or two when the girls would take one look and paste themselves to him. But she'd always finally put the worry aside. Cousin Emery doted on his parents as she did hers: proprietarily. He would tend himself sensibly, but he would always, foremost, see to them.

Aunt Lil sat at one end, Uncle Anson the other. Beside Lil was Ruby, looking striking and tired, as usual. Ruby worked at an office downtown to pay the bills she shared with Evan. She wrote, she said, in the cracks of that. She was Claudia's height and wore her wavy hair bobbed. And though she embraced the others warmly, Ruby always seemed after that a touch removed from the goings-on as if turning over some unrelated, private problem while she watched and listened. Evan beside her looked cheerful, fresh, and restless, as usual. A genial, sturdy man with auburn hair in the style of the actor Gabriel Byrne and rich brown eyes, he edited college textbooks for a big firm back east. After twenty years he could do it sleeping, he said, and was impatient to travel. He had a grown son who lived in Iowa now. Ruby had never had children. The two had met between acts of a play in the city, been married nearly a decade. They seemed to fit; balanced each other out. Sara thought them the smartest couple she knew; Evan could be especially funny.

Colin called out from the kitchen like a film director. "Places, everyone!"

They assembled. Anson raised his wineglass. "*Iechyd da,*" he declared. The Welsh toast.

"Skol, Cheers, Santé," sang the others. The bells of crystal touched.

Evan mugged in his Scottish thug accent. "Och! Ye'll *naught* be servin' the *Welsh* crap, will ye!"

Laughter; chatter; clinking silver against china. Food apportioned. Compliments tendered. More wine; more toasting. Emery excused himself as soon as he'd cleaned his plate to return to his computer game upstairs, and the group began to talk of Colin's life on board the ship.

Ruby was curious. "What is it like, to be at work where it's a constant party?"

"Fine," said Colin. "We work hard but the atmosphere's merry. People cut you a lot of slack when they're on holiday; they only want a bit of help having their fun. I can fix almost any drink you name now. Try me!"

The women, gaily taking the bait, tossed elaborate drink names at him and Colin recited the ingredients rapidfire. The women laughed and clapped and corrected him when they remembered differently, and then the other women argued what they remembered, shouting over one another. The men silently wondered where this skill would take the boy in ten or twenty years.

"Do you not get claustrophobic?" Ruby asked after the jovial drink-naming had waned.

"Not at all," Colin shrugged. "There are stops onshore, y'know. And oh, do I get the exercise!" He rolled his eyes. "You'd not believe how fast we have to run. How much to do."

Sara, softened further by wine, watched her temporary beau. His good manners and boyish sincerity reflected well on her, like the glow of the candles. Her hand held up her creamy, plumpish cheek, which had grown pinker.

Evan rumbled. "*I* want to go on a cruise"—here the other men echoed: "Hear, hear—yeah, right! Me, too!"

"—but Ruby won't let me."

The men chorused: "Whoa, hey, bad, Ruby! Why not?"

Ruby smiled. "I don't *let* or not *let* anybody," she said, modulating so her meaning might be clear to their listeners, on the heels of his words. "It just seems—not something I'd like. You're caught in this small space, and all you can do is make noise at other people and stare at naked sunburnt bodies 'round the pool and eat and eat and drink and drink—"

At "naked bodies" the adults stiffened for a beat.

"And the problem would be?" Evan asked, eyes blinking wide in wonderment.

Everyone laughed, relieved.

"Gout!" replied Ruby. More laughter around the table.

"But there'd be this confinedness to it, wouldn't there?" Ruby said after a minute. The table quieted again. "It would become a kind of floating prison. Nowhere to escape: you'd be stranded. You'd have to eat what they gave you and buy what they sold, at their prices. And hey: what about that—the expense of it, huh?"

Ruby had seized at the money aspect—Sara saw it took the heat off her, stopped her having to explain herself further. And sure enough, as soon as Ruby said *expense*, all the men's eyebrows lifted and sank together; they nodded, grave as pallbearers. Expense was their constant stalker, an ongoing haunting. At once the talk veered into the costs of things, which proceeded into costs of local real estate, then what various jobs paid, and finally what predator, or gang of them, or fatal historic trend, was responsible for it all.

Claudia placed her hands at table's edge and leaned toward Aunt Lily. Her wide turquoise eyes were deliberate, and so was her low voice. "Our cue, Dear."

Aunt Lil and Sara's mother Claudia hated it when the men talked of money, though both felt they should try to understand it. For their husbands, trying to talk to them about it was like trying to bathe a cat: each would momentarily appear to stand still for it but bolted at first chance. Now the two women exchanged a look and rose to clear the entrée dishes. Each of them balanced stacks expertly, hauling them backward through the swinging door into the kitchen.

Ruby and Sara remained at the table, although they, too, were bored to stupefaction by the money talk. It always led to the same conclusions, Sara thought: there's never enough, nothing's fair, and it's all getting worse very fast. Ruby crossed her eyes a quick second at Sara in dramatized solidarity, and Sara grimaced back. But then Sara remembered that Ruby had deliberately set the fellows on that trail, like hounds on a fox.

Colin poked his head through the back-and-forth door to announce pie and coffee; Uncle Anson strode to the liquor cabinet to fetch brandy and liqueurs. Sara excused herself and ducked through the swinging door to help Colin slice the three pies and plop whipped cream onto each piece. She found her mother and Lil side-by-side at the double sink, busily hand-washing everything and never quite completely rinsing the stuff: a vexing British habit her mother had unthinkingly adopted from being around Aunt Lil so much. It always rankled Sara a little and made her worry about diarrhea. But she kissed her mother's silky cheek, which smelled of bluebell cologne, and then she kissed Aunt Lil's, which smelled like pie and fresh dish suds. "Wonderful meal, Lala," she murmured.

Lil turned her face to smile at the girl. "Ah, you're always welcome, darling; anyway it was all our Colin's doing, eh?—*Colin, we loved it,*" she lifted her head to call the praise to where her nephew stood across the counter. He grinned and continued grinning down at the milk he was pouring into a little pitcher. Sara came up behind him and kissed him last. "Hey, Queenie," he whispered.

When Sara emerged through the swinging door back into the dining room, the conversation had switched again.

Evan was talking. "It's the best education a young person can have," he said. "I've told *you* so, haven't I, Sara." He addressed her the moment she appeared, plates stacked three to a hand and slightly up each forearm, waitress-style: mince, pumpkin, apple pie.

"Told me what?" Sara lifted her face and brows in polite inquiry as she allowed her Uncle Anson, who was nearest at hand, to rescue pie-laden plates from her arms one by one, an acrobat's pyramid disassembling.

"Travel. That the minute you can, you should take some time to get out of Dodge," Evan said. "You learn everything that way. Right?" He beamed at her. Evan was always confident— maybe it was a by-product of editing, which gave him the last word. The families relished Evan's energy. He could be categorical, convinced of his rightness—but he was guaranteed to be colorful.

Sara smiled at Evan. "Of course," she said. She took it as assumed she would have her turn at traveling. Next summer, probably. Evan was going to help her plan it. To Wales of course, to see the Talbot relatives. Maybe Colin? And then maybe to Malaysia.

"Damn straight." Uncle Anson's gallantry was alcohol-warmed. He only needed a cherrywood pipe between his teeth, Sara mused: *Great American Uncle*. He stood at table's head, handing out plates of pie. "Best damn thing a young person can do, before they get strapped in. We all did it ourselves one time or another, eh lads?"

Stephen's face, looking up from his dessert, was in a familiar bunch-up, as if about to sneeze. Uh-oh, thought Sara, here it comes. How her father loved to take exception! It was his way, she supposed, of saying *I'm here*. You could time it. Let everyone else agree and it wouldn't be three beats until Stephen Bream's objection rose. Sara knew her father as generous; she hadn't yet comprehended how piercingly he envied her education. He threw words out almost blindly, like long fishing lines, casting for stimulation, for ideas.

"It's different today," Stephen insisted. He ran a hand past his ear. "More difficult. The young person's got to make responsible preparations for such a trip, hasn't she." Stephen's elfin voice had a way of making suggestions sound like conclusions; like he was thoughtfully leaning across your lap, cutting up your food for you.

"She's got to study up on where she's going, and she's got to earn some of the spending money," he said. (Sara took note of the *some of*, both blessing her father and sighing for him. It was Stephen who went around turning off all the lights, who checked the thermostat was never a hair above 65, who used the dinner candles down to thumb-joint-sized stumps.) "And the young person's got to file a flight plan, y'see, and know what'll be expected of her in various places. And she's got to call home at intervals. The world's too rough."

"Bollux," answered Evan flatly, borrowing Uncle Anson's brisk expletive. Sara could never remember if it meant buttocks, or balls, or poop. It sounded like all of them.

"A person's got to throw some things in a bag and just *go*," Evan said. "Yes of course, have some money and some maps. But the rest should be allowed to just happen as it will; that's the joy of it, see? Why, we did that, Ruby and I, wandered around Europe when we both got some time off last year, didn't we, Roo. And we're not even kids anymore." His face and body turned slightly toward her as if offering his wife the podium, urging her, wholesomely, to testify.

Ruby had been quiet. She looked at Evan with a faint smile. There was affection in it that seemed wrought, like maple syrup dripped from a long tap.

"Yes, we did," she answered softly.

"And we got some fine adventures out of it, didn't we," he pressed. "The trains! Now there's the way. European trains have everything over on us. They go everywhere. Young people crawling all over 'em. Cheap, affordable. You buy a pass, go wherever. And the characters!" he said. "The cross-section, heh Roo? The stories!"

Ruby seemed a bit quieter than usual.

"Yes, the stories," she said. She had leaned back in her seat, looking at Evan.

The women had returned from the kitchen, glancing quickly at Ruby as they took their seats, an anxious light flicking briefly in their eyes. They gazed immediately down at their desserts. Colin was still buzzing in and out, the swinging door going *whappa, whappa.* Aunt Lil had put the FM radio on. The group could faintly hear something symphonic as they attacked their pie. Uncle Anson was already pouring shot-sized goblets of liqueurs and brandy.

Evan was saying: "Those stations, especially. Train stations were always a scene. Each one different. Dramas of all sorts."

Suddenly he looked at Ruby. "Remember that one—the blonde woman? at the station?"

Ruby looked back at him. Her face had acquired an odd look—sort of slowly incredulous.

"I remember," Ruby answered him in a careful, queer voice.

"Tell it," Ruby added. Her tone and face had about them, Sara thought, a whiff of dare, or curiosity.

The group had stilled. Claudia and Aunt Lil each looked quickly up from their plates a scant second and lowered their eyes at once.

Evan's face, too, wore a strange expression. Curiosity was in it. Curiosity, and a sort of savoring. Evan seemed to want to give Ruby something he knew she wanted, but he also seemed, somehow—interested in how she'd handle it. This observation flashed only an instant in Sara's conscious perception, like sub-liminal advertising. Then she promptly forgot it.

"You tell it," he said to her. He said it calmly.

Ruby gazed at him, then around the table at her dinner-mates. She seemed to be gathering herself; a sort of bracing.

"We were in the train station—I can't remember where." She shook off, like a pestering moth, the annoyance of not being able to get the place right. "Maybe Prague. But it wasn't a glam-orous place; it was someplace out of the way and poor, where people were kind of unwell and beaten-down."

Ruby recrossed her legs, tightening their lock and pressing them back under her chair. Ruby was in her late forties, but Sara thought she carried it well. She wore a black cotton sweater and straight gray skirt, and small, thick, silver loop earrings. She stretched her spine forward as she began, forearms on the table, gazing at her interlaced fingers.

"There was a woman, in the station. The waiting area. American. Youngish, maybe late twenties. She was tall, big-boned, with long, dry, bleach-blonde hair. Her face was not beautiful, I remember. It was more like a mug. She had a bulb nose, like a clown nose. Her eyes were nice, I guess. Blue."

Ruby inhaled, looking at none of them. She appeared to be watching an invisible television screen and describing what she saw happening there.

"The blonde also had a friend with her, a girl, scrawny and plain-looking, with dark, curly brown hair. The friend seemed to be the blonde woman's escort or slave or something." Ruby flicked one hand off to the side. "The one that tags along. The *valet*," she said in a little burst, as if relieved to have located and loosed the desired word.

"But the thing about the blonde woman," she continued. "She had these enormous breasts. Way out of proportion to the rest of her. *Enormous.* And she deliberately showcased them. She wore a tight, striped T-shirt with a low, scooped neck. And tight Levi cut-offs, hip-hugging. There was no way *not* to see her. This—apparition. You all know the type. With this huge—shelf. It went in front of her like a neon sign. Like a wheelbarrow."

The room had grown very still, though the symphonic march was still pounding witlessly from the speakers. Sara glanced automatically at the men. The older men's eyes had gone a bit glassy; their features assumed a slack, scrupulous neutrality. Aunt Lily and her mother looked openly pained, their faces cinched with sad, resigned attentiveness, like a therapy group's.

Colin was silently tucking furtive pieces of pie into his mouth.

"It's a type," Ruby was repeating. "A nearly universal type. The stripper type. Hooker-with-heart-of-gold. Or heart of lead. Who knew what kind of heart this woman had, or whether she *had* a heart. All that mattered, really, was the shelf. And the hair, and the tight Daisy Mae clothing. She knew she had the shelf. And she had decided to dress this way to tell the world—for whatever reasons—hey, take a look. Take a good, *long* look."

Ruby seemed not to be seeing the assembled company anymore, though she still looked around at them somewhat suspiciously—as if they'd all perhaps somehow helped effect what she had seen. But her eyes, a hazel-brown mixture, were filmic, inward.

Anson finally cleared his throat. "Ruby, this is a somewhat common—I mean, what exactly was—"

"Here was the thing," Ruby interrupted fast, like a hand smacking down. "*Every single woman* who saw the big-breasted blonde, immediately looked angry or sad or disapproving. Every single woman. And Evan here noticed that fact. Immediately."

Ruby glanced for a microsecond at the general outline of her husband, whose face now matched the strange, inchoate blankness of the other men around the table. Sara tried to recall Evan's facial expression a few minutes earlier when he had urged Ruby to tell all this in the first place. Had a gleam of titillation flitted across it, like the shadow of a bat? Something hungry and sly?

"It was Evan who pointed this fact out to me. *Look at the faces of all the women who see her*, he told me."

Sara glanced in a kind of terror toward Evan. He now appeared to gravely rue whatever impulse had launched this recounting: a dignified statesman into whose lap someone has just quietly emptied a glass of cold wine.

"And it was true," Ruby was saying. "Wherever the blonde went, in the station and then on the train, as she sauntered down the aisle to choose her seat, with her—her—consort," Ruby's voice seemed to surge and thicken. "She left this *wake*: a sea of female faces watching in anguish. Including me. Including me.

"And of course," Ruby added from her thickened throat, "the male faces were all following her, too. Oh, yes! But they didn't respond like the women did, no, no. The men, you see, could only be—"

Ruby paused. "—*delighted.*"

Stephen interjected quietly. "This is something we all see from time to time. What was it about this particular—why are you choosing," he faltered. The rest of the men sat wordless. The women kept silent, never taking their eyes from Ruby.

Everyone had stopped eating pie.

Ruby leaned forward again. She had a shiny table knife in both her hands which she kept twisting, its face turning up and down so that fake-chandelier light bounced off it rhythmically. "Because Evan" (she jerked her head slightly to her left toward him: he didn't move or look at her) "was trying that day to suggest to me that—all those watching women being sour like that—was the result of their own stupidity, their own narrowness, their own ugly prudish provincialism. It was some failure of imagination on their parts. Small and petty and jealous. They were disallowing erotic freedom!" panted Ruby.

"Do you see?" she implored her company.

A tableful of faces stared back at her. The room was fixed, airless. Sara felt her breath lodged behind her solar plexus. She wished her Feminist Studies instructor were at the table just now.

The silence hung over them.

"OK. *Why* would all those women be angry or sad or sour," Ruby coached her listeners, like a teacher whose class is so unwarrantedly dim she sees she will have to drag them by the hair up the staircase of reasoning, step for step. "Why would all those women look unhappy?" she asked again.

Sara moved her bottom a little on the woven cane seat of the dining chair, wondering whether she should know the answer or whether the question was a trick one. She felt full and sleepy and a little cross. How had this started, anyway? She wished she could fast-forward it; have a nap. Colin was staring gauzily at his fourth piece of pie. His skin wore a greasy sheen; his eyes had gone dim and focusless. He looked vacant and dense all of a sudden. Maybe she wouldn't stop off to see him on her way to Malaysia.

"Because all those women can't look like the Breast Lady! They can only look like the kind of woman they are! Fat skinny, old young, purple or green, whatever sad little breasts they were born with! Or maybe they've actually lost a breast or two! And so *why*, my friends, should they *want* to look like Breast Lady? Can you tell me that?"

Her mute audience squinted, their faces pinched. Ruby answered herself in a trembling, singsong-patient voice.

"*Because that is what men want.* So what we have here, my friends, is the fucking saddest, unfairest thing on earth. It means there's *no exit*, do you see?"

Ruby seemed to be pleading with them.

"You *know* you can't look like the Breast Lady. Men *want* you to look that way. The one who *does* manage to look that way is the winner—" Ruby mumbled an aside to herself. "For the moment anyway, until she gets old, or until better breasts come along."

She turned back toward her listeners. "Meantime, the rest of us are shit. We're mud. We're gonna have to crawl through the pathetic remainder of our lives like lizard scum, not daring to look into anybody's eyes. Because we're *irregular goods*, see? Mongrels. We don't measure up; we don't rate. And this is all—this whole business—old as Solomon, old as Solomon, do you see? There were always wives, and there were always dancing girls, weren't there?"

Ruby didn't wait anymore for an answer.

"But Evan here was smug. He was superior. Because he was proving the wretched puniness and spitefulness of women's minds. They couldn't allow the stripper type to have her glorious day. And he himself, and all the other men—no matter what they look like—get to enjoy hell out of the spectacle while feeling superior to it! It's airtight, y'see? Seamless! The men can look and look—and we're the shit of the arrangement—"

Ruby stopped, breathing hard. She looked panicked, like she'd come to the edge of a cliff. Like she wanted to sweep the table of all its china.

Sara wondered idly what it was like at home between Evan and Ruby. What it would be like for them driving home tonight. She tried again in her mind to piece together what Ruby was saying, but it seemed to come apart in chunks. Sara loved her Feminist Studies class, but that felt more like a glossary of vocabulary terms than anything Ruby was raving about. And everyone at Oberlin was so hyperconscious of not stepping past any harassment bounds and all. People walked each other back to their dorm rooms at night, and there were emergency Campus Patrol phones everywhere with special blue lights over them, and free condoms given out in all the campus restrooms, even at the bookstore. And the entire student body and faculty were issued thick looseleaf-binders of rules about inappropriate touching. She felt she should jump in and reassure Ruby, but she could not think what to say. Sara could hardly imagine her own parents having sex, frankly; when she tried to it made her a little sick.

No one spoke.

Evan was inspecting the crumbs on his dessert saucer. His face was tired and embarrassed. Too late, said his face. Mistake, mistake, said his face.

Another long silence. Ruby held fistfuls of the draped tablecloth in her lap.

"Aw, c'mon, Ruby," Uncle Anson finally said in his earnest lumberjack way. "It's just a thing that happens. It doesn't need to wreck your life. Besides, lots of men out there—in here—love their wives, really. Are faithful to them. All their lives."

Ruby didn't answer. She was slumping. But her eyes still shone, a wild tension in them that seemed to barely gag the reply she desired to make to Anson. Maybe Ruby was thinking *yes, but it's Breast Lady you always want: her you'd always go to if you could get away with it; her you fantasize when you fuck your wives.*

Why were Ruby's nails always so *untended*, Sara heard herself noticing in the silence that followed. They were healthy enough in the ovals of their deep pink beds, but their edges were invariably broken and jagged. Could poor Ruby never find time to pick up a file and shape them? Hands were so—*public*. Sara spread her own hands noiselessly on her lap: they were soft and full as pale, dimpled puppies. She bent her head to examine them critically. The iridescent blue polish had been a good choice. She wondered whether fantasizing about a stripper was the worst thing a man could do. Really, the whole question was silly: Sara honestly couldn't conceive what man would choose a stripper over herself. And whyever would she bother with one who did?

"Pictionary, anyone?" Aunt Lil warbled suddenly in a too-loud, Eleanor Roosevelt voice. It was the two families' longtime custom after dinner.

"Me!" came Emery's buoyant voice from the second floor. Emery loved Pictionary because he often won. He did this by wedging himself closest to the easel while the teams were guessing, and staring hard at the drawing and the partly constructed word. This blocked everyone's view and caused a lot of irritated complaints. Thank goodness the boy'd been upstairs out of earshot just now, thought Sara. Or had he?

"I'm up for it—*aherck!*—up for it!" Colin blurted in a falsetto high as Mickey Mouse's; he blushed, hocking harshly in his throat and reasserting at a lower octave. *A kid,* Sara thought wonderingly. *A kid on vacation.*

"We've got to get going, I think," Evan said in matter of fact tones. "Work tomorrow and all. Let's go, Roo."

Ruby sat, still clenching the tablecloth draping in her lap, a fistful in each hand.

"Yes," she said absently. She rose, and in that gesture Sara saw a terrible exhaustion. Sara remembered that Ruby once told her that she rarely got enough sleep and that she envied people who could. Was it from too many jobs? From her and Evan having trouble? Did they still love each other? Would they break up? Sara roved her mind back over the faces and sounds at dinner tonight. And for an unnameable moment she glimpsed her own long life to come: an infinite corridor of such dinners. Two soldierly lines of them like upright video cartridges packed in rows fanning back to the horizon. It occurred then to Sara with a tremor that whatever you saw of people during all those dinners might never—never, in your whole life—offer the scarcest representative sliver of who they were. You were only touching the tippest-tops of them. Icebergs. Great jagged hulking ones plunging down and down, God-knew-how-far. And God knew what was actually frozen in their blueblack depths.

Evan had found their coats and tucked Ruby's around her. She submitted with almost no motion. Sara couldn't help thinking of television comedy satires of the soul singer James Brown, led away by his "handlers" from a draining performance with a cape tossed over his sagged shoulders.

Evan went to shake hands and kiss everyone goodbye, while Ruby waited blank at the door. Sara stepped quickly over to her, taking both her hands. They were clammy.

"Ruby, thank you for coming. I—I want you to know I'll be thinking about—what you were saying tonight," she stammered.

Ruby looked at the girl's soft, open face, her flushed, flawless skin with its fine blonde down, her blue eyes clear.

"Yes," Ruby said. "Or maybe it won't—I don't know," she stopped herself. Her own tired eyes—their importuning message trapped there like some mute exile's—filmed momentarily with a weak warmth.

"You're so lovely, Sara." It came out like a beseeching: *How will you save yourself?*

Sara gazed into Ruby's face. *N-slash-A*, she was thinking. *Not Applicable here. It's a new day, Ruby!* Emboldened by the largeness of her vision, her fondness surged. She felt maternal, solicitous, pressing Ruby's hands together between both her own.

"Ruby, promise to get lots of rest now," she said.

Evan stepped forward, bussed Sara on the cheek, thanked her and the others again, and, his hand dutiful at the small of Ruby's back, propelled her gently out into the spicy-cold November night. Sara shut the door behind them and stood still. Through the door she heard a great heaving sob outside. "I'm sorry," she heard Ruby's voice cry sawingly and low. "Sorry, sorry," the voice sobbed, the crying now more muffled, as if into a coat. Hiccoughed words. "They're just good people. They're only good people." And then Evan's tones, indistinct but soothing and patient, smoothing down the weeping, smoothing the hoarse words. Smoothing it all over as both their voices receded down the street into the early dark.

Sara stood a moment staring at the lacquered oak grain of the Talbots' closed front door. Abruptly she turned and leaned her back against the door. She breathed in deeply and exhaled hard, so her eager bosom rose and fell in its China-blue sweater. She looked at the assembled company in the living room. The men were standing, hands in pockets. The women sat on the couch, hands laced between their knees. They watched her.

"Well!" said Sara, resonant and bright, pushing off from the door and sweeping forward into the room. She stopped and looked at them with a wide smile, from face to face.

"What's next!" Sara clapped her hands and held them clasped there before her in a prayerful beat: the long, gathering moment before a choral director strikes her hands high, and, letting them fall, commences her music.

BETTING ON MEN

Carver hadn't arrived yet that morning. Carver was always a couple of hours late, unless he was up to something, as Malcolm liked to say—so Malcolm took the opportunity to stick his head inside Bridget's office door.

"I may as well give you some news you won't like." His eyes bulged, a light she'd learned to recognize. He had information that would bear on her.

"Oh?" Bridget's heart stiffened, though her face assumed its Casually Yet Responsibly Amused look. Formed in a stroke. *Never be caught out of character.*

"What's up?" Voice bright, brisk. *Please just go away.*

It was not yet eight in the morning. Bridget had mastered the habit of arriving early, because she knew Malcolm would trudge up the stairs and see her settled at her desk. Malcolm set great store by such habits—early arrival, crisp dressing, neat workspace—the whole Andrew Carnegie rigmarole. Malcolm noticed, kept track, never forgot. He bought motivational books and videotapes, titles like *Play to Win*. Wore a jacket and tie each day, never took lunch, carried a heavy black three-ring binder in which every element of his present and future were plotted. Bridget knew Malcolm took the binder with him on vacation. Bridget also knew (he found ways to let it drop) that Malcolm rose at four in the morning to meditate upon his goals, enter them into that binder. One day she'd found it open on his desk. On every other page, amid the appointments in Malcolm's neat, square print, she also saw—flipping forward, backward—these carefully copied lines:

> *What are the facts?*
> *What do you think?*
> *How do you know?*

Below them, an apparent breakdown of Malcolm's waking hours:

> *.4 professional*
> *.1 family*
> *.1 exercise*
> *.2 spiritual*
> *.2 self-improvement*

After she saw those pages Bridget stumbled back to her own desk, dazed. She'd felt then as though she and all the others in the building were made of Gumby clay, living in a Gumby world. Furniture, cars, food—the entire earth, the wretched and the royal, the infinite universe and its boiling suns—Gumby-stuff, spatulate and squishy. She'd rummaged in her drawer until she found a chocolate cookie, taken small, careful bites, cupping a hand to catch the crumbs. She chewed slowly. Dark, sandy sweetness melted along her teeth into the slick membrane of her mouth's inner walls, infusing butterfat, cocoa, sugar. A tiny sigh escaped her. Still chewing, she threw the crumbs into the far back of her mouth as if they were aspirin, stared damply out her office window onto the empty street below.

Optical-Consolidated made coatings and filters for eyeglass lenses and medical equipment (applications for car windshields, computer screens, paints, plastics), and business in the last few years had shifted to warp speed. The headquarters where Bridget worked had set up several more production plants around the state. Bridget knew nothing about window films and light-interference pigments, but she didn't need to. Checks poured in through the daily mail that Bridget stamped and photocopied and stuffed into a depository bag (zipped sturdily, click-locked with a key). She added them first on the calculator: rich, threshing sounds, totaled with a chewy flourish. Those checks added up to more money any single day than anyone who worked for Opti-Con—excepting Carver, the owner, who was a millionaire—would ever see in their lifetimes. It did strange things to you to see that much money every day. Bridget talked to herself about it. *Twenty round-the-world cruises. Five medical-school educations. Homes. Cars. Land, clothing, food.* Even so, the checks Bridget handled seemed unreal. Play money. (Though Carver's platinum Jaguar and Malcolm's espresso Mercedes stood real enough, sleek as small aircraft, gleaming in the parking lot amid the scuffed sedans and trucks.) In fact very little seemed real to Bridget during office hours except the gauzy light through her second-story window, the soft sounds of cars and trucks passing below, the low hum of the computer's hard drive, the degree of comfort in her lower womb relative to how recently she'd emptied her bladder. A nest of swallows had built itself near the outside corner of her window—a dozen of them actually, conical clay masses made of thousands of beak-sized scraps of dung-colored mud, wedged under the building's eaves. A perfect bird-sized hole punctured the crown of each like an amphora, a feather or sprig of straw drooping out. Early mornings in spring Bridget watched the birds jet back and forth in round wide arcs like those whirling swings at the fair: feeding babies, fortifying nests (bits of mud, pass after pass), a chorus of clickings and murmurings as they swooped. This would enchant Bridget—until a ragged commotion set up when the birds fought. The angry chatter exploding in a linear rush like a string of firecrackers, the compact bodies dive-bombing their rivals, the furious blur as warriors faced off, hovering mid-air—chastened her. All was not nice, in birdland.

Carver Hammond had been a young university dropout when he took over the modest operation, bequeathed by his retiring parents. Now Carver's gold-foil business card announced him Chief Executive Officer. Malcolm and Bridget had been recruited, with dozens of others, in rapid order. The situation began harmlessly enough.

They all do, at first.

"These are the file systems." The young woman who'd trained her had waved her hand like a quiz-show hostess toward wall after wall of cabinets. Bridget's heart had sunk through the floor as she'd nodded. Here was the great lie, the great dysfunction. *You had to pretend you liked it, and you had to pretend you cared.* All her life Bridget had managed to sell herself to jobs like these, sending ahead a resumé of useable skills like itemized portable attachments. In four years Bridget had connived a way of working at Opti-Con which dwelt on the surface of her own awareness, a rosy skin of apparent attentiveness that never betrayed the truth: that she could never, in any part of her, take business posturings seriously. That despite the cheery noise they made, neither she nor her co-workers cared if they ever saw each other again. That if a paycheck could be deposited to her bank without her having to leave home, she'd rig that in a blink. A lifetime of such jobs had distilled Bridget's thinking to the simplest of longings:

To be left alone.

To read under a tree, the Japanese maple in the yard behind her cottage, an in-law unit with window-boxes. Bridget had rented all her days. When her father died everything was left to her stepmother, a peevish woman who'd loathed Bridget. Bridget fled home at seventeen, eked an A.A. equivalent at the local university, then knocked around, keeping afloat as salesclerk, typist, waitress, now administrative assistant—what the British call a *dog's body*. Three husbands had appeared in stately succession, each of whom she had duly assisted: from each she had either resigned, or been fired. Counterculture children all, a gardener, a carpenter, a café socialist. None had owned property, none had money. There was one grown stepson, a directory assistance operator up in Oregon. Bridget wondered why it had taken her so long to grasp that the marriage model itself was—God help her—another business to run.

When Carver made Malcolm Chief Financial Officer, Bridget had agreed to serve as Malcolm's assistant in exchange for a raise, and an office of her own. The private office freed her for the first time from the slave-work of the front desk. And the extra money made it possible to save—perhaps enough, one day, for a down payment on a small mobile home. True, her office was directly beside Malcom's, and true, a special door fed between the two rooms so Malcolm could stroll in at any time. To her relief, Malcolm kept that door closed.

In exchange, though, Bridget had to endure Malcom's terrible habit.

Malcolm spent the days buttonholing employees with vicious gossip—mostly about Carver, whom he hated, but also about other employees. Lamenting to each that he was buried with difficult, exacting work, Malcolm made his rounds—Human Resources, Controller, Order Processing—plying these people with bilious rumors. Employees quickly understood he took nourishment from the habit: lip-smacking *dolorosa*.

And this morning?

"There will be fireworks today," Malcolm intoned, staring at her. It was his No Good Can Come Of This look, and it contained unmistakable relish. Never in her life had Bridget known anyone to take such pleasure from doom mongering. Maybe it was kin to ambulance chasing.

"What exactly are you—what are *we*—expecting?" Bridget asked. The hatred and distrust between Malcolm Lowe and Carver Hammond had been racing along like black mold. Malcolm loathed his chief, Bridget knew, because Carver had inherited a *nouveau riche* adulthood—wore aloha shirts to work, joined expensive tennis clubs, took his wife to Paris for dinner. Like other wealthy men (Bridget had worked for two), Carver pored over every tiny charge on credit card bills with mulish suspicion. Malcolm, on the other hand, was from the deep South, progeny of a drunkard father and a mother who'd simply disappeared. Malcom had done time in the Army; worked as a salesman for pre-fab houses before hooking the Opti-Con job.

Now the two men were corporate officers with six-figure salaries, and Bridget was their *admin*, necessary and generic as a plumbing fixture. It amused Bridget she might actually have married the fellows she served, had she but played the game— worn seed-pearl chokers, gone to certain parties. In their youths Bridget and Carver might have crossed paths on the same campus. Carver would have been cutting classes to hurry to rehearsal of a blues band he'd started, stopping en route to hock his parents' stereo speakers. Bridget would be returning to her au pair job from the university's library carrel, books clutched to her pounding heart—having written a poem to the handsome young student she'd admired at an adjacent table. She'd left it there for him while he'd gone to the bathroom, then fled. Malcolm, meanwhile, would have been marching in stifling heat over Alabama dirt, bearing a sixty-pound pack and a rifle amid moving planks of other sweating men kitted up the same way, lifting their boots to the hoarse, rhythmic shouting of a superior officer. A few years later Malcolm would be standing at the check-in desk of a Holiday Inn, raincoat folded over a suitcase-toting forearm, the other arm pressing a copy of *Think Your Way to Fabulous Success* against his side.

But why, Bridget wondered, did Malcolm stay at Opti-Con if the very sight of Carver—his spiky hair and restless gray eyes, his stocky swagger, shoulder-clapping *camaraderie*, chewing food with his mouth open, interrupting again and again to insist on some embarrassingly specious point—why stay on as Malcom did, if Carver infuriated him so?

For that matter, why did Bridget herself stay on?

It wasn't complicated. Opti-Con paid well. Better than any other work available to a woman with Bridget's unremarkable education—far better than teaching school, for example. It was late to train for anything new; training required time and money. And it cost such energy. All that theater, that *presenting*. The older Bridget got, the more difficult presenting became. Harder to suppress the urge to laugh at these blinkered little zealots. Their comic solemnity. Their meetings—my God, their meetings. Their infernal, brainwashed *pep*. Admitting of no past, only the frantic present, waving the blueprints about. *Going forward*, they called it. Bridget shook her head. The child's obligation to attend school became an adult worklife that became, inevitably, an albatross that began to reek. Should she be ashamed for wishing only to read, to water geraniums? Wasn't that why people played lotteries?

As to Malcolm's reason for staying—Opti-Con was worth millions now. *Fortune* Magazine listed it. Carver was on the screen, a *player*, having to enlist a battery of CPAs and lawyers to shield his income from rapacious taxes. He liked trying to get Ted Turner or Bill Gates on the phone, certain they would be pleased to hear his thoughts. Every few months he made Bridget send them little gifts (good cigars, fountain pens, grappa in cut-glass bottles) with roguish personal notes from him, and every few months had to be satisfied when Gates's or Turner's secretaries sent an icy thank-you back to Bridget.

When Malcolm left Opti-Con, Bridget saw, he wasn't about to do it with nothing in his hands besides the receding warmth of a firm handshake.

Carver—who'd wakened slowly to the fact that his quiet, hound-faced CFO actually despised his every breath, and planned to demand a cut—was now positioning his own cannons. Both men had hired attorneys. Both avoided one another in the halls. Each addressed Bridget with a curt message for the other, the way divorcing parents might address a child seated midway between them at a long table: *Tell your mother to pass the salt. Tell your father I suggest he obtain the salt by his own means.*

Bridget soaked in a shallow bath every morning (poached front and back) to soften her nerves, a steaming washcloth over her face to steam out ill will. Driving off from her cottage fragrant and moist, thermal mug of strong coffee in the dashboard's plastic holder, she would listen to the classics station, feel momentarily soothed. Opti-Con headquartered in the countryside near dairy and livestock farms; each day as she drove Bridget could roam her eyes over green hills and pastures, gamboling calves, lambs. Flocks of starlings lifted and cascaded to *Sleeper, Awake* or the *Pastorale*, and Bridget would sigh. *How lovely the wild mustard in the green fields.* But within minutes of arrival at the hangar-shaped plant her stomach would tighten, her shoulders start to harden into a sort of iron T-bar.

"He's pulled something," Malcolm said now, jerking his head toward their chief's still-locked office. "It marks the last straw."

As usual, Bridget fastened her innocent gaze to his, her cheeks and eyes and forehead coagulated into sympathetic attention. How else to respond? What would Malcolm do if he knew her thoughts—murderously weary, drained to the bone, bored to gibbering by his spiteful, oldwomanish act? His Rasputin campaign, contaminating every day by scarcely eight in the morning. How often had Bridget wanted to plead *for God's sake, give it a rest.* How often had she burst from the building, stood heaving lungfuls of cool air—to replace all the breath sucked from her, those hours upon days upon years of listening, nodding, making inane gabble? Her head rang with noise, falsity. It built up over years, she thought. Like birdshit.

Can you believe what Carver's done now? Malcolm's voice, low and urgent. *Taking the whole place down with him this way? a faithful team like you and me?* It was sticky, that implied moment of intimate conjugality: *you and me.* Sticky as flypaper. Because no sooner had Malcolm left your office than he'd visit another worker down the hall, telling tales on *you* in there. Like the course of any poison, it had visible effect. Employees were forced to listen, to agree and agree. Soon they began to ache all over with an unredressed feeling, like a low-grade virus. They felt like sheep who'd let themselves—*baa-ing* obligingly—be herded and gouged and bled.

Oh, but how they needed that paycheck.

They walked around staring at one another in a vapor of toxic bewilderment.

Malcolm lowered his voice now. "Carver wants sole signatory approval of checks going out. This, on top of the extra audits and inventories. It's an insult to my office, and I won't have it," he said.

Again Bridget heard the sensual relish. It made her think of words like *impeachment, court-martial.*

Malcolm folded his arms. "I've seen an attorney who's advised me that I have a good case. And that everything Carver says to me now should be documented," he said with thick satisfaction.

"So if he tries to talk to me, I may have to ask you to take notes," he added, watching her.

Here it was, then. His trump.

"Ah," Bridget said, her mind shrieking, flinging itself bloodily against her skull as her face kept itself stretched into a blank moon of sympathy. "Notes."

"Think you can handle that?" His face telegraphed its odd mix of triumph, token solicitousness, stealthy curiosity. Malcolm liked measuring her reactions to his news, to gage the veracity of his own hunches. Of course Malcolm didn't really value Bridget's opinions, except as they confirmed his own. And of course Bridget lied like a pimp—with a sincerity that amazed even her. Bizarrely, Bridget found her sympathies malleable. She could turn a dial, lock on, absorb the world Malcolm wished to represent. Project it completely, speak its language. Reflect back wholesale his rendition of things. Worse, some part of her *wanted* Malcolm to feel validated, knowing perfectly well his projection was Gumby clay. Wanted him to find whatever in hell it was the poor fuck needed, though he made five times her salary and would kick her prone body aside to get it. Deep at her center, Bridget *wanted happiness* for this sad, twisted creature who was paid too much to do too little, who cultivated people's misfortunes the way others crochet, who counted his own wildly inadvertent good luck as the direct result of copying dime-store tenets from motivational speakers into a zippered black binder.

Worse still: when Carver cornered Bridget in a similar session of opinion-harvesting, she found herself warmly attending *his* every signal. *She wanted the same happiness for Carver.* Carver in his bermudas and flip-flops, his breezy *howareyou* not a question. Yet Carver also grinned, told jokes, brought strawberries, chocolate, flowers. Transparent condescensions to be sure, paving his road to Rome—but his eagerness, against all logic, touched you. Some part of Carver was still a vain boy, playing air-guitar to impress girls at parties. That was the part Bridget rushed to reassure. Sometimes Bridget was afraid her surface-self had become so adept at this witless will-to-good it would finally swallow up her real self, like a sleeping-bag turned inside-out. What drove this reflex? Estrogen? Husband-helping? Bridget was forty-eight. *When did you get to stop doing this?*

Of the two in her office that minute—Malcolm leaning morosely against her doorframe, herself perched at the desk, hands laced with alert, phony attention—one would retire on a fat chunk of severance pay, and one would not. Retire: meaning no more 6 a.m. *dee-dee-dee-deep* alarm, dissolving cottony dreams. No more scrounging for a piece of stale bread and mottled apple in the fridge so you wouldn't spend money you didn't have on lunch. No more fishing in the black jungle of the closet for clothing that did not bind or scratch or make you look like one of those listless women pushing a cart down fluorescent K-Mart aisles. No entering the office burning-eyed at 7:50 a.m.—turning on copiers, starting coffee, trashing last night's junk faxes.

No more feeling your heart and stomach drop, to see Malcolm's baleful figure slowly mounting the stairs.

No more wincing at passing inmates, seeing them wince back.

No. Bridget was sentenced to work at jobs like this for the rest of her life, to make enough money to live. Answering to men like Malcolm, who trotted myths of themselves before them like religious effigies in processionals. She would have to pander and lie to men she pitied and deplored—for a barely sufficient wage. But Bridget had done it for so long that some part of her also still imagined—*why? why?*—that whatever she said to these men, whatever she did for them, might finally count. Add up. Gather some karmic reward. On her tombstone, perhaps? *She'd Like to Buy the World a Coke?*

"I'm a big girl, Malcolm, and this is part of my job." Bridget felt her face form its competent smile. A dangerous, precipitous edge of some sort was approaching. She must take special care now not to fall in.

She held the smile steady. She was surely losing her mind. "I guess I can do what I'm asked," she added, with warm huskiness. *You and me. You and me.*

She would do what she always did: Say yes to everything. Keep mentally bundled, let conflicts roll past far above her as if she were watching from the bottom of a clear lake: a bottle-colored ceiling where light played through its roiling surface. She bent over her own daily list. Call the landscaper. Wire money to the tax board. Cancel the contract for linen delivery, renew the bottled water contract. Deliver financial statements to the bank—the bank which was nervously floating millions to Opti-Con, based on the millions the place was attracting. Fantastic, this financing game, the betting it represented. Men betting on men: a wondrous cantilevered tower, greed multiplying on itself, metastasizing out and out into raw untried space. Yes, it was still a male bastion. Because the men craved this stuff like sex, craved the taste and smell. It stirred and spurred them. The bulletins, indicators. A cresting wave you rode. Magically coming into existence with the advent of the business day, magically ceasing at five o'clock Friday—though if big dollars were at stake the men would stay up all night, fly around the world, change diapers if need be. They were young, these grinning bankers who came around. Young but not looking well, with blue cheeks and white flesh that slumped a little over starchy collars. Their handshakes were strong enough to bring water to your eyes, their own eyes brightly hard. The words they spoke were also brightly hard. Sometimes their breath was bad. When she smiled and shook hands with the bankers, trying not to breathe the smell of their awful breath, Bridget thought of a scene in *The Magic Christian*, elegant financiers in suits and bowler hats wading into a tank of raw sewage to retrieve the dollar bills scattered over its surface.

She heard familiar voices rising.

Carver's shadow had flicked past her door, striding into Malcolm's office. Bridget heard their voices spark.

Oh, no. Here it comes.

In a moment Malcolm opened Bridget's private door. He didn't knock.

"Bridget, can you come in here, please."

Dear Lord. No time to think. Get up. Get up.

She seized her pad and pen, walked to the doorway between her office and Malcolm's, backed herself gingerly against its frame. Carver stood facing Malcolm's desk, arms folded, legs wide apart. Malcolm sat behind his desk with his hands in his lap and his head retracted at the neck, eyelids flicking. Both men were pale.

She held the notebook before her, looked from one to the other.

"I want a tape recorder," Bridget announced as she shoved her way past the heavy glass door into the tiny electronics store. It was the first such store she had spotted from her car. "For my office. On my company's credit card."

"Okay," nodded the saleswoman. She was a large, older matron whose box-shaped bottom swayed in tent-like pants. Her quick eyes studied Bridget's, made the mental leap: if the credit card is good, ask no questions.

"I want a good one. The kind that picks up voices nearby. The kind you don't have to bend down and yell into," Bridget said, her voice loud and trembling. The only other customer in the place, a woman with a gray ponytail and straw hat, looked up.

"Fine," agreed the matron, turning back around to bob from side to side toward the display case behind the sales counter.

"I want the batteries that go with it, loaded into it right here, please. And lots of extra batteries," commanded Bridget like a bank robber.

"Right-ee-o." The matron lifted down a machine the size of a lunchbox. She placed it on the glass counter with a pack of batteries; excused herself to find more in the back room.

Bridget scanned the store. Lit plastic 7-Up signs crammed against reading lamps, radios, extension cords, CD storage cases, kiddie nightlights. A half-dozen televisions sat along shelves opposite her, one switched on, sound conveniently muted. It was tuned to a travel channel.

The gray-ponytailed woman resumed browsing the jostling oddities: clip-on book-lights, coin-sorters. A plastic trout lit up and sang when she pressed a button, mouth clacking open and shut. The expensive things, from which the tape-recorder had been extracted, stashed on shelves behind the counter— more difficult to shoplift, Bridget guessed, her stomach taut. The late morning shone whitely through the front window, the rest of humanity at that hour meek and enchained at an office or classroom desk—misting produce or washing glasses or making beds. The heedless white morning pulsed into the store like a laughing crazy whore: the morning would be anybody's, for the moment, who could afford her.

Malcolm had announced to Carver, as Bridget stood in the doorway that morning like a trapped hostage: "My attorney has advised me that from here on out, anytime you talk to me, someone should be present to take notes."

Carver hadn't flinched from his wide-legged, arms-folded stance.

His mouth twitched at its corners, a perceptible sneer. With effort he reorganized his face to express longsuffering, restrained, ironic patience.

"Fine with me," he said evenly.

Carver would never express surprise, for that would be to admit imperfect control. He took on his pained-diplomat voice.

"But you know, Malcolm, what a shame this is. What a shame. If ever there were anything you needed to say, you know my office door is always open."

This was a lie. Carver's office door was sealed shut most of the time, because he was on the phone trying to sell the entire operation for two hundred fifty million dollars, and everyone knew it. Everyone pretended not to know it, to humor Carver and keep their jobs. The buyers appeared to be a consortium from Diamond County to the south: a half-dozen young men and one woman with severe, expensive haircuts, dressed in wrinkled black linen. Some wore wire-rim spectacles. They'd looked about twelve years old as they toured the place, staring at Bridget and the other middle-aged sheep grazing blankly in their offices along the upper and lower hallways. Carver's whiffing the big money was painful to see: he'd led the group around like a NASA director, gesturing. Already he planned his speaking tour. He'd keep a private jet, several homes in different countries, a few million in trust for each of his three highly irritable young children, Ariana, Joshua, and Zeke. Door open or closed, Carver was fused to the phone, brokering, bartering, bluffing. You could hear him if the door was open, interrupting people by loudly repeating a single phrase. *But what I'm saying/what I'm saying/what I'm saying is/you've got to/you've got to/you've got to.* Louder and louder, til the other speaker had to give up, let Carver speak. And because Carver was owner, because he had the money, no one—save his wife, a trust-fund heiress and the only other person on planet Earth in a position to do it—could tell him to go fuck himself.

Bridget scribbled as fast as her hand could go.

"You have specifically instructed an employee that all checks be routed for your signature," Malcolm said. "And you have overridden my express wishes against another round of inventories and audits."

"That is my right," Carver answered coolly. Bridget knew these activities prepared the company for a sale. She moved pen across paper faster.

"These are insults to my office and my responsibility," Malcolm said. "According to my attorney—"

Carver cut him off.

"As owner I have the right to call these shots. It has nothing to do with undermining—"

"That's your creation," Malcolm said.

"Malcolm, the money! There had to be a way for me to see what was going out!"

"Get it done then, Carver," Malcolm said quietly. "Get the place sold. You've marched your buyers through here often enough. People aren't stupid, and your pretending doesn't make them—"

Carver went a bit yellow.

"That is between my attorneys and me! I have the right to work on this in total privacy. I do not have to disclose it to you or anyone else unless I actually have—"

"That's one spin to put on it," Malcolm noted.

"Malcolm, Diamondhead has not offered yet! We are trying to come to an agreement. This is tough!"

"My understanding is you've made it tougher by doubling the asking price. What I'm saying," Malcolm added as Carver went paler still and opened his mouth, "is if Diamondhead is ready to go, why not get it over with?"

"I won't rush it," Carver said fiercely. "It's very difficult to focus when every day I come in and another maneuver has been made without my—"

"I think you're pointing the finger in the wrong direction," Malcolm said. "There should be an atmosphere of trust here. People just want to come and do their work and go home. Right now," he said, "they feel like meat in a butcher's display case."

Bridget felt a force field expanding from Malcom's desk like a hot, clear balloon. She wanted to cover her ears.

"These are not simple documents. There's a lot at stake," Carver said.

Boy, *was* there, she thought. But only one man would collect those spoils, and they all knew it. They also knew that Opti-Con had flourished despite Carver, never because of him. He gave useless orders; squandered money on limousines, spas, air-ionizers; bragged, complained, offended people. He was the founder's son.

"I'm trying like hell to resolve this," Carver was saying. "And *I'm trying to take you with me*, Malcolm."

Carver inflected this the way parents spell c-a-n-d-y in front of a toddler. He gazed meaningfully at Malcom.

Ho, thought Bridget as she scribbled. *Take this purse filled with gold for your troubles, my good man*. Here was Malcolm's off-ramp.

"All I'm asking is you do your job," Carver continued, softly now.

"I made a mistake with the checks. But I'm coming off this charged atmosphere. These incendiary stories. You have turned my employees against me, Malcolm. There is a trail of ugly stories I follow and it leads back to Malcolm Lowe.

"You've even turned Bridget against me," he said, his chin thrusting up.

Malcolm's eyebrows lifted a notch. Both men turned to look at her.

Bridget's writing stopped. A bolt shot through her.

"Have I done that, Bridget?" Malcolm asked.

Bridget's threw her eyes out the window. Morning light swathed the street. A school bus trundled past, and a pickup truck piled with green blocks of hay. Two dogs pranced smiling, followed by an elderly couple. A young woman pushed a stroller. Men and women and children, calm, unafflicted, living their lives apart from this antler-lock caging her. Lives concerned with honorable trivia. Groceries, lawns, mail.

"Listen," Bridget began. Her mucousy throat gurgled the word. She cleared it strenuously.

"Listen, you guys, this can't be about me! I only want to do my work and not be put in anybody's camp. That's all I want, I swear." Her face burned.

Malcolm, pleased with this vague echo of his party line, looked back to Carver, who stood, arms folded, legs apart—the way Superman stands when ordinary mortals try shooting at him with ordinary bullets.

"Of course you do," Carver snarled at Bridget.

Abruptly he turned back to Malcolm. The rest of the staff were toilet paper, but Malcolm ran the numbers. Carver spoke with something close to tenderness.

"Malcolm, I agree this is nonsense. Believe me, I want it over as much as you."

"We're all anxious for resolution," Malcolm sniffed.

Bridget noted the *we*. What *we*, she wondered.

"One baby step at a time," Carver crooned. "Have lunch with me today, Malcolm. We'll hammer at it."

He means, thought Bridget, hammer it out.

Bridget leaned heavily against the glass countertop.

She let her eyes do the easy thing—drift to the television screen.

The travel channel camera panned over a harbor, perhaps Burma, somewhere steaming and green and very poor, a grimy harbor rusting with old cargo liners. Then the camera moved out from the harbor, the water sewer brown. A small barque came in view, pushed by a young man in rags. He worked the boat's pushing-pole with a foot, one arm clinging to the craft's makeshift mast; the other dragged a fishing net. His movements were lopsided, automatic, well-practiced.

Then the scene changed: a building project on a wet mountainside. Narrow terraces were being cut; along these, skinny workers covered in mud moved rocks and boulders off to a pile. Perhaps they were making a road. The camera zoomed in on the men's bare legs and feet, placed carefully on mud as they hauled the stones, balancing loads on heads or shoulders, dumping them finally off a shallow embankment. The men's faces wore an impenetrable fatalism. Some were boys. All sharply thin, smeared with sweat, yellow-brown mud. A harried busyness about the masses of them, including those who seemed to boss them. All evinced little thought other than to keep the sodden mess moving, rippling and staggering the cargo along in their bare hands the way crumbs of food are moved by ants.

Bridget's knees trembled. Her stomach twisted on itself: she pressed it harder against the counter. She wanted to fly out of the store into the harsh white sky, shamed to the soles of her feet. Her feet! Smooth and clean and pinkly nourished, feet that only went bare when she swam or bathed, padded on cool lawns in a suburban yard or park. She wanted to go back to the Opti-Con office and take the two men by their collars, drag them the length of the highway to the airport. Stuff them into a cargo carrier; fly them to the Burmese building site. Strip them to their shorts. Away with the thick wallets, the glistening Rolexes, the heavy gold rings, away with the keys to the silver Jag and es-presso Mercedes, the Italian shoes, the zippered three-ring binder, the Palm Pilot, the Diet Cokes, moisturizing face-spray. Prod them forward into the mud-splashed, empty-faced, milling lines of stone-carriers. Carver and Malcolm would carry boul-ders and branches and sticky detritus of wet, steaming earth from earliest light until dark, when they would be given a small bowl of white rice. They would sleep on a mat of woven reeds if they were lucky, otherwise they would sleep on the mud itself. Mud they would be forced to excavate, live in, breathe and eat and shit in and be coated with, mud that would grind deeply into every pore and crevice of them, their anuses, pubic hair, their ears, each of their torn fingernails and splitting toenails, their eyes and scalps and mouths and down their throats, cover them for the rest of their wretched and pointless and queerly ab-breviated lives.

Mud that would never, ever wash away.

"Thank you," Bridget croaked to the saleswoman who'd placed in Bridget's hands the brown plastic bag, weighty with the expensive machine inside, the machine loaded, poised to record the human voice. The plastic bag crinkled importantly. Bridget took a last look at the silent television. Swarms of thin men and boys struggled, with resigned vacantness, against the sopping earth. Holding her package from underneath with both hands, Bridget found her way to the shop's door, began to shoulder through. As she emerged her eyes floated up without purpose, so that quite by accident they caught sight of the eaves under the little store's roof.

She saw the swallows' nests, and remembered.

Tiny. Tireless. Ferociously building their hive-like fortresses, back and forth, with mud. Bits upon bits, pass after pass. Heedless persistence. Hierarchies of power, space. Sudden avalanches of chatter: furious, symphonic fights. Disappearing in afternoon to sleep, so they could begin it all again.

All was not nice, in birdland.

There was a curious calm in it, if you relinquished feeling you had to personally account for it. If you gave up the fraying hope that it not end badly, you got back something. Something that placed you again in the present, rolled the odometer back to zero, let you recommence making your way. Why this was so, she couldn't immediately say. But it was. Slowly, Bridget stepped clear of the store's entrance, let go of the opened door. Blinking, looking about, she walked into the whitely-lit noon; walked from one world back into that from which she'd come, into the given day with her burden.

REARVIEW

Her father and stepmother work as teachers, count themselves enlightened, throw cocktail parties. In Drew's mind they form a dim, scrolling backdrop, like repeating film of landscape and shrubbery. Drew likes being left to herself, steeped in the dreams and confusions of the young, cocooned in winter by delta fog. She listens to Gregorian chants, the Modern Jazz Quartet, *Fanny*; she lights candles, believes in a parallel universe where everything makes perfect sense if she can only find a way to pop through to it, escape once for all her Sacramento suburb. The givens of family, she sees at fifteen, are imposed without logic, arbitrary as space debris falling on you from the sky. She keeps herself in a state of readiness.

Her stepmother, Hazel, has produced from prior life a daughter, Carrie, nineteen, who has come to live with Drew's family after getting herself into trouble elsewhere. What kind of trouble is never specified, at least not to Drew, but at some point words pass through the air over Drew's head, about keeping bad company. At the beginning Drew likes to lean against the bathroom doorway, early mornings, watching Carrie apply makeup.

Drew has sometimes glimpsed her stepmother doing the same, through the half-open door to her parents' bedroom. Across long years the vision will pop forth: cold pearl light from the window, Hazel sitting motionless in her slip at a vanity mirror, lightbulbs framing it like a movie star's, her back to Drew, stockinged feet flat on the carpet. It is the feet, and the face in the mirror—a nude socket like a mannequin's, as if waiting for an expression to be applied—something dead in it, the unspoken caption *So it's come to this*—that frightens Drew. Carrie, on the other hand, chatters away while she dabs and smooths. Drew assumes Carrie copies makeup techniques from her mother—since Carrie also copies Hazel's haughty, tailored look, even sneaks Hazel's clothes from her closet (triggering a salvo of yells, sending Drew scurrying to her room, her father to his den in the converted garage). The clothing the two women fight over—clingy knit ensembles that require dry-cleaning—seems alien to Drew, who wears cotton shifts, black leotards, A-line skirts. Drew takes modern dance, makes wide queenly arms, stretches a long back to *Jesu, Joy of Man's Desiring*. She can no more wish to look like her stepmother than she can want to look like the actress Jane Wyman, whom her stepmother resembles with her short, dyed-red curls. Drew wants to look like Janet Margolin in *David and Lisa*—and she actually does: dark hair in a pageboy, dark eyes. Carrie, for all her efforts, resembles no one—except when she paints her lipstick's outline larger than her lips, it gives a drag queen effect. Drew would never suggest this—what a drag queen does or is, still murky to her.

Carrie always stations a cup of milky coffee at the corner of the bathroom sink: it cools while she works, the cup's rim imprinted with a cracked apron of coral lipstick. Over the mirror the fluorescent tube hums, casting morguish light. Liquid foundation turns Carrie's face and neck brownish orange, erasing brows and lashes. Then powder, from a compact. Next comes blush, dusted on with a stubby brush. (She waggles the brush at Drew's nose; it makes a sneezy, perfumey smell; Drew shakes her face like a dog.) Then eyeshadow, black eyeliner Cleopatra-thick, then mascara (eyes bugged wide). Sadly, Carrie cannot be called pretty. Her nose and chin are sharp, her pale eyes squinty, set at a plaintive angle. Yet her face becomes striking with the laying-on of paints and powders, and her personality too alters before Drew's eyes. The crayoned brows rise, the gray eyes surge. In fact the makeup seems to stoke Carrie's resolve from within; at the end she blazes as if gripped by revelation: *I'm onto things. I've figured it out.* Even her voice changes—arid, an elevated state of being. Drew watches hypnotized, a tiny ball of dismay in her stomach. After the beehive hair is teased and smoothed, the sticky, metallic-smelling spray swirled over it like anointing mist, Carrie steps back and whirls to face Drew: one foot forward, slightly turned out, hand on hip. A matador, a model. *Well?* her exalted carriage inquires. Eyes flaring, face muscles glued into their new alacrity, Carrie looms: surely about to do something fearsome—maybe star in something.

In truth she is about to drive three blocks to the community college, where she is taking Psych 101 and Business English, part of the reform deal cut with Drew's parents.

Which is where Carrie meets Joey.

And is creamed by him. Rendered watery, like whey. She brings him home: at the entrance to the kitchen stands a black-haired James Dean. Slender, pale, eyes the blue of winter sky. The blueblack cast of the beard beneath the skin of his cheeks and chin, no matter how closely shaved, frames the tender wound of his mouth. His smile gives out a sweetness like nothing Drew has seen—a kind of helpless radiant crumpling, the way a baby breaks into mirth. A complete giving over in that smile, all the elements of the self conceded—a haplessness almost feminine. Drew stares at Joey Kavanagh when he first appears, as though he wears antennae.

She will remember little else about that day. She will remember all five stood awkwardly in the kitchen, her father seeming to shrink to the edge of the picture, keeping himself at the margin with a glazed, distracted air, like a chauffeur who does not wish to peer too closely at the doings of his passengers. She remembers Carrie holding Joey's upper arm with both hands, levering him by turns toward each of them.

"This is my mother, and my stepfather. And this is my little sister."

Joey's long frame tilts forward. His eyes offer wet mute awe, and a hand extends, dark hair on the back of it. Drew clasps it so numbly she cannot later remember having done so, or whether the hand was cool or warm, dry or damp. She continues to stare, shocked by the naked sweetness tracing the lean face, the winterblue eyes open and believing.

After that day, understandably, Carrie becomes scarce. When Drew does catch sight of her stepsister, Carrie is a perfumed blur (Tabu or Je Reviens), preparing to go out with Joey. The little bedroom Drew's parents have given Carrie at the back of the house becomes a staging area, discarded outfits flung across the bed or balled up on the floor. Few comments are made about the evolution of the obvious. Perhaps Hazel and Sid have no energy to interfere. Perhaps they consider the romance wholesome, compared with whatever Carrie had got up to before. The family must piece together what little Carrie has told them—all she herself knows. He's come from Canada, taken odd jobs. No mention of relatives. Where does he live? No one's saying. Wandered into the community college. Seeking what? Something about computers, something about guitars. (Computers in this era are mainframes the size of outbuildings, attended by men in lab coats.) Carrie rushes the information, because of course what can it matter. Joey in his leather jacket, his jeans, his raw, broken smile?

A distance of many years lets what was mysterious fall together, like parachutists joining hands midair. Much later Drew will understand the lonely young starveling's confusion, true of any stray—his throttled, trembling gladness to be taken in by a pair of fragrant breasts, a clean warm house full of food and wine, himself the center of a group of eyes, civilized voices petting him. What extra thought can it need to let oneself swim into determined arms, rest against the bulging bosom, accept the glass of Sangria, the plates of baked chicken, mashed potatoes, bowls of chili, corn bread, green beans with bacon, Spanish rice? Might he care for some chocolate ice cream? We have syrup, if you want.

Yet Joey seems petrified, every visit. He strains to follow each least remark, falls over himself passing butter, answers questions in a soft panic. It makes Drew ache to see him sitting like a polite android across the shiny countertop where the family takes meals, concentrating on their gestures and tones as if their language is foreign. Carrie flanks her lover tightly at the table, speaks for him when he struggles for words. Glancing from each to each, Drew tries to imagine what it is between Joey and Carrie. Despite his hollow look he is gentle as a petal, as if any slight would score his cheeks. When Carrie tells gross jokes, her words loud and coarse, Joey lowers his head, smiles in mortification. And what about sex? Drew has no real experience herself, but she pictures the couple twined, writhing in the narrow bed of Carrie's room, maybe on a pallet in Joey's rented room, if he has one. Maybe there is nowhere to writhe but the back seat of his dusty blue Plymouth. The words *Carrie must feast on him* swim beneath Drew's confusion like the wavering outline of a big fish.

When one March evening after dinner her parents summon her to a family council, Drew's stomach drops. Family council means one thing: Hazel wants something, and Drew's father will go along with it. Carrie happens to be home that night, a rare change—and she looks ill, Drew notes, watching her stepsister enter the living room. Carrie wears sneakers, jeans, an olive-green sweatshirt. Slouching, her face chalky— no kin to the laquered apparition before the bathroom mirror. Maybe Carrie is being grounded, Drew thinks, though she knows Carrie is a bit old for that. A cold night, February. Drew perches at the edge of the ottoman, her face a practiced mask of alert neutrality, hands loose between her knees. The formality of rituals embarrasses her. Adult notions in general torment her. She knows Hazel is pleased with the concept *family council*, knows her stepmother brags about it elsewhere. Drew longs for the invisible trap door to fall open into the parallel world. Carrie slumps on a stool by the kitchen counter. Hazel has taken Sid's armchair.

Sid stands by the gas fireplace, its two false logs gray from repeated cooking. Hands in trouser pockets, eyes on the weak blue flames. They make a *shhhhh* sound. When everyone goes to bed, Drew knows, her father will sit watching the fire, as if waiting for the flames to spell an answer to something he has asked. Hazel clears her throat, addresses Drew.

"Carrie is going to have a baby. Your father and I are prepared to see her through it. She will stay with us until the baby comes, after which she and Joey will find a place."

Drew's face is a moon. Carrie stares at the carpet, Sid at the whispering fire.

"Um, wow. I guess—congratulations?" Drew looks from face to face, coming to rest on the pale, sullen form in its olive sweatshirt.

Carrie shrugs and tries to smile, with lopsided result. Hazel chews her lip; Sid watches the blue feathers of flame.

From a distance of years, months are nothing. Months are minutes, if that. In about five minutes—so it seems—Carrie is a zeppelin. All her body has swelled, concentrating its forward ballast at the middle: her great belly jutting before her as if she is bearing a torpedo under her tent shirts. She finishes her classes, cleans her room, empties the trash. Her eyes hold a different light: softer, diffuse, comically apologetic.

Joey still comes to the house for dinner, but less often. When he does Carrie still makes a show of crude jokes at the table, many about the enormous belly preceding her, and again Joey lowers his face and smiles in terror at his food.

Drew views these changes from a vague, incurious distance, having retreated into the floating dream of her days. She waits at the top of the street for the school bus, turns in her homework; her teachers, relieved and tired, praise her. She reads *Giovanni's Room* and *Catcher*; she reads *Death in Venice* and *Cress Delahanty*. There is a line in *Giovanni's Room* which electrifies and sickens her, something like *you know very well what can happen between us*. She tries to banish the line. She eats apples and boiled eggs and sunflower seeds because she wants to be thin, the thinner the better, likes the feel of her hipbones jutting, her clothes hanging more and more airily around her limbs. She waits for the invisible trap door to give way to a world of mist-garlanded castles, cottages beside clear brooks, and a young man who will stride toward her smiling, hoist her weightless form in his arms and carry her, bride-over-threshold style, into the sea.

Her stepmother and father keep their rounds, but seem to have less to do with one another. They seldom argue in front of her, but some days Drew comes home from school to Hazel slamming cupboard doors, lips pressed together. In the background Sid's face holds a familiar, ironic grimness: he is drinking. Drew never wants to know why they fight or how much anyone drinks; she wishes it would all fix itself or become—distant, at least. She loves her father so much it trusses her up inside, but Hazel's sour watchfulness weighs on them all like a rain-soaked tarp. Hazel had once been an older student of Sid's. Panhandle born, her red hair, movie star makeup, vodka-fueled conversation passing as a sophisticate's, had brought him down hard. Drew assumes her stepmother has hauled her life up from a world of sagging porches, smells of washwater, bowls of mush. But that was *then*, Drew reasons. Hazel's dank ways confound her—it's as if she hates joy, won't allow for it. Lately Hazel goes out by herself many evenings, and Drew finds her father glassy-eyed in his throne opposite the fire, a tumbler of yeasty scotch or bourbon in one of the hands stretched forward, Lincoln-style, on the chair arms. In the days her father was courting Hazel, Drew remembers, the two had sat before the fire together evenings in armchairs side by side, hands held across the armrests, two glasses of wine on the hearth: from the stereo Tony Bennett sang "Once Upon a Time" in an echoey voice. Though the scene made her queasy (she would back away silently to her room), Drew had checked her twelve-year-old self fiercely: it was good, she told herself, that her father had found someone to love.

When Sid is drinking these days, however, she doesn't like to be around. He wears a small, maniacal smile then, as though he understands something fiendishly, sorrowfully funny. His eyes are unbearable. Drew fades back into the hall and disappears.

Other seasons march through the valley, of course: delicate springs with pastures of tiny yellow and pink wildflowers, brilliant new grass along the creeks. Hell-hot summers that burn your skin like paste. Late, warm autumns, their lush roses, chestnuts and maples purple and gold, persimmons like lanterns. But the whole of this account arrives fixed, for some reason, in perpetual winter; its movements wind out like a clock beneath the layer of freezing fog. Perhaps memory and weather collude. In any case what next emerges from those cold clouds is a fat baby girl, brought home one afternoon in Carrie's arms.

The chubby face is a lucky blend of its mother's gray eyes and (when the baby smiles) its father's sweetness. Standing in the same spot at the mouth of the kitchen where Joey was first introduced, Carrie, weeping, places the swaddled infant in Hazel's arms, whose own face struggles briefly with something complicated. Sid looks on, invisible, from the other side. For some reason Joey is not among them that day. Perhaps he has found a job, and is working. Drew watches the momentous handing-over, the baby chunky and pink. Carrie names her Ella.

Things get more difficult after that, and more confusing. The baby lives in the house with all of them, Drew, Carrie, Hazel and Sid, while Joey does not much appear. No one tells Drew what this revised arrangement means, or what its duration will be. If discussions take place, they do so behind bedroom doors or while Drew is at school. No family councils are called. A lot of hasty motion fills the house, no longer a staging area for Carrie's dates but instead, unsurprisingly, for response to the baby's needs. Drew is at school all day, by night completing homework or reading in her room, so she does not often see the others except at meals, which happen more haphazardly, in shifts. Carrie takes catnaps when the baby does. She is quiet, emptied, not barking coarse jokes. Her face is scrubbed. She wears jeans and men's shirts.

"Sorry, Drewie. 'Scuse me, hon." Her stepsister crashes into Drew rounding the corner into the hall or the kitchen: Carrie races back and forth preparing bottles, fetching clean diapers, folding laundry. When the baby's wails ring through the house, Carrie runs faster. Drew holds the baby on occasion, but she is not drawn to the fleshy package, and doesn't like when the baby smells in ways babies periodically can't help but smell.

Joey, meantime, seems never there.

In late winter of her senior year, Drew is sitting in French class droning *des saucisses, sans doute* when she is called from the room by the principal, a man she's rarely seen. Ray Hutchins's office is smaller than she has imagined, musty with carbon paper and mimeograph ink, desk untidy with folders. He has an exhausted face, skin like dark red leather. "You need to go home today," he says. "Your stepsister is on the phone." He gestures toward the black receiver, which Drew only now notices lying face-down on the messy desk, tethered by its curly black cord. Mr. Hutchins exits his own office, closes the door. Drew's heart is beating hard as she picks up the heavy receiver, a dense black bone.

Carrie's voice is high-pitched, slow, careful. "Drewie? Drewie girl, you need to be strong now. Are you listening? Drewie, something has happened. Your dad has died, Drewie. He had a heart attack. I'm coming to pick you up now, Drewie."

Drew waits alone in front of the school. The unfamiliar truancy—standing outside the school in the middle of a wan afternoon, cement walkways vacant, frigid air so quiet—as stunning as the inability to understand what Carrie has told her. She shivers, hugging her books. When Carrie drives up, her face is pale and streaked. The baby is with Hazel, who was also sent home early. Carrie embraces Drew with fleshy arms, smelling faintly of milk.

"How is Hazel?" Drew asks. She asks not because she cares but because some dull awareness prompts it: Sid might have liked her to ask. She will not remember Carrie's answer, or much of what follows. A service is arranged at the Unitarian Church. Someone plays "Sarabanda" on guitar. Someone speaks, words that will not stick to any part of thinking or memory. Drew sits in a row of folding chairs between Hazel and Joey. On Joey's other side (on the aisle, in case she has to get up quickly) Carrie shushes the whimpering baby, fluffing her up and down in little shakes as you might shake water from a colander. Joey has placed an arm around each stepsister at both his sides, his head bowed. Drew can sense this: the side of her eyeball knows that Joey stares at his lap, though she cannot look at him directly or at anything but her own lap, because of crying. She has to clench her teeth to keep from making what would be horrible noises. But the feel of Joey's arm over her shoulders makes a small thrilling current inside Drew, though she cannot stop crying. She knows she looks ugly, her nose engorged and running, the tissue in her hands reduced to soggy fibers, her cheeks and eyelids swollen, sticky. When it is time to stand and walk from the room she rues the loss of that arm over her shoulders, a warm cloak stripped away. She cannot speak to people who approach her in the parking lot. Standing miserably before her, they tell her what a good man Sid was, what Sid meant, what Sid gave them. She stares at the asphalt, seeing wisps of her father's thinning hair blowing in the wind, his lifeless cheeks and nose, perhaps colored greenish gray. She imagines this because she has not seen, will never see: Sid is ashes now, traveling by train to Colorado, to go into the earth at the base of a hill beside his brother and mother. Drew nods, crying, watering the pebbled asphalt of the church parking lot.

They are driven home. People arrive. Someone has arranged food along the kitchen counter, the counter where the family has always taken meals. Someone has started the automatic coffeepot, which makes swoosh swoosh noises while brown liquid floods the clear cap at its peak. Crackers and cheese, sliced apples, cookies. The apples' white flesh shows a network of brown veins. Hazel moves like a pope in the midst of a buttressing entourage. She seats herself at the far end of the counter; the entourage stands back of her, conferring; she begins stuffing crackers and cheese into her mouth very fast.

Hazel is furious at Sid for dying. Her locked face says so. It is the ultimate insult, thoughtless, inconvenient. Intent, puffy with anger, she eats.

Drew stands by the gurgling coffeepot; her eyes wander the countertop to its opposite end, where a white business envelope is propped against the sugar bowl, the envelope not sealed but agape like a fishmouth. She leans to peep inside it.

A man's wedding ring and wristwatch, cloudy metal against white paper.

"Drew."

Joey, beside her, peers down into her face. Carrie has gone to the back of the house to settle the baby for a nap. This can take time; Ella is a fusser.

Drew lifts her gaze, looks into eyes lit like ice at twilight: clear, whiteblue. The silken mouth doesn't know what to do with itself, the long cheeks bathed in five o'clock shadows.

"Drew, is there anything." His voice a murmur, as if still inside the Unitarian service. He means, *that I can do.* Her perception floats outside itself above her left ear, at about the level of the smoke vent for the gas range behind her, invisible disembodied mind filming the two of them. Joey's thumbs are hooked in his pockets. He's still wearing his leather jacket.

The living room has filled with guests; like a seeping tint they begin to cover visible surfaces, massed in groups, sitting, smoking, flowing through the glass doors to the screened patio, the white day outside like cotton batting. Sussurating voices, louder as more appear, clinkings of cups and glasses and silver, smells of cologne and aftershave, cigarettes, coffee and sweet rolls, just as if a Sunday service has given over to a potluck reception. Somewhere in the middle of all of it, Hazel eats.

"Can we go somewhere," Drew hears herself say. Some separate, instant calibration appends a safeguarding cover:

"I should drive; follow me in your car."

Drew drives now, it is legal at sixteen, a used, pea-soup colored Volkswagen beetle, an early gift for her pending graduation, from Sid. He has also given her his Royal portable typewriter, in its own hard shell case. She loves the typewriter, feels it to be a little time machine on which she might print a ticket to the future. She had flung her arms around his tired neck: "Thank you, Daddy."

"Yes," Joey is saying. He makes his way out. Drew gives him a minute's lead, moves to the hall closet, extracts her coat. No one notices in the packed, noisy rooms. When Drew shuts the front door behind her, pausing in the sheltered portico, she is only able to orient a fragment of sight—so many cars, parked up and down the street—before Joey is blacking out vision, taking her in his arms, almost lifting her from the ground as he kisses her.

No, not here. But against logic, against reason, against wits she is lost, the mouth sliced peaches, roughness of the emerging beard, skin scented with the room they've just left and something deeper all his own, homey and sugary like cookie-dough; for long moments she dissolves in darkness, feels her body pressing against his tall form, something hard there at the middle of it, insisting.

Blind, she pulls back, turns, takes long steps to her car, breath shallow from her nostrils, with shaking hands finds the ignition, turns her key, backs into the street, swings toward the highway.

He climbs into his Plymouth, and as she accelerates she can see him pull out—his hands working the wheel fast, one over the other—his car falls in behind her, its front grill, chrome eyes in her rearview.

What has happened, what has happened. She wants to look at her own face in the rearview mirror now, wants to see her eyes—she fully expects they have turned orange, pulsing, pupils shaped like a cat's—but if she checks her eyes in the rearview he will see her doing that. Her mouth still tingles, scraped by the rough cheeks, wet from his lips and tongue, cookie scent still in her nostrils, her body subsiding from the arch it had known to assume. Between her legs aches slightly, thwarted, bewildered.

You know very well what can happen between us.

She merges with the freeway, glancing surreptitiously as she can at the rearview: the old Plymouth clambering into traffic behind. It is a dust-covered blue; never will she forget that blue surface, its curves, chrome grill like a manic grin.

She is heading north toward the foothills, joining early Friday commuters fleeing the city to mountain weekends, or to homes dotting pastureland. Old barns ratchet past, fruit stands, farm equipment. She holds the wheel, stares forward. The moisture of the kiss has dried from her lips; they feel nude, exposed. Joey's car peeks from behind the car behind her; she can see him, every few minutes, edging the Plymouth slightly wide of the blocking vehicle to keep sight of her.

Oh, God oh God. Words stream through, or rather, inchoate air where words should be, circling and circling, trapped behind her eyes. *Where am I taking us? What will we do when we get there?* Her eyes see the wild oaks, the gas stations, the billboard for the steak house owned by the football player, the daylight white powder sifting through the air. She is sixteen years old, her eyes roving familiar signs for cattle auctions, casinos in the Sierras, parcels of land for sale—her eyes unable to stop checking the rearview, her chest caught, clenching. Who knows how long the whole business takes? She can measure it if she wants some day, the distance in miles from the on-ramp to the unexpected exit; divide that total by the car's speed. No help now: all she can grasp in this span—minutes, an eternity—is a queer reversal. Beautiful Joey, urgent in the rearview, does not look beautiful anymore. She can see his knuckles, his determined squint. *God, God.* Beautiful Joey, strings of black hair falling greasily over his forehead, grimacing against the pale afternoon, urging his old car to catch up, looks pathetic. Looks small. Looks like some scruffy nameless *shmo*: some sad, scared, lonely loser amid the squadron bearing down, enmeshing him.

Why and *how* do not connect these bulletins in Drew's sickened teenaged gut, as the engines about her roar. Only comprehension, and its sturdy accompanist, shame. God forgive me please. Daddy forgive me please.

Only after she has grown quite old will it occur: *Carrie forgive me, please.*

Without signaling Drew makes a lunge for a sudden exit, Rocklin, the base of the foothills. At once the driver behind her slams his horn, its enraged howl dying like a train's as the aggrieved driver flies on. Her wild turn, the maddened car immediately back of her, a matter of seconds—much too quick for Joey to react. In horror she wills herself not to look back as she maneuvers, frantically, to slow herself around the immediate hairpin of the off-ramp: as if she has led him to plunge from a cliff she wills herself not to see him speeding helplessly on, trapped in the barreling commuters. Heart juddering, hands icy, she wheels the few weedy blocks to the freeway's entrance in the other direction, and on the approach, guns it; the pea-soup-colored beetle merges with a metal armada rolling south, whence she came.

She drives and drives: through Rio Linda, Land Park, through the mannered Victorian neighborhoods downtown, til daylight fades. After dark she parks on K Street, walks past lit shop windows, neon clubs, hamburgers and onions frying in open nooks. She buys a hamburger; it tastes so heavenly she wolfs it as she walks, licks the waxed paper. Polished jalopies tool past, motors glub-glubbing; people stroll in groups, smoking, laughing. She dawdles until she grows chilled, her legs heavy. When she arrives home late that evening—a house of women now, all asleep—she slips into her room, curls up beneath the quilts without undressing.

As best she can recall, Joey was not heard from after that day; as if by silent assent no one spoke of him. Drew never inquired, never volunteered. She might or might not, in those years, have been surprised to learn that after a lifetime, the memory would exhume itself. No way to know back then, naturally. Only time provides some kind of shape and, of its sort, order. The players would go their ways: Hazel institutionalized for dementia (blank, smiling, a compliant little girl); Carrie to a marriage, another child, divorce, and retirement with a woman; the children absorbed seamlessly into their grown lives' work and worry like rain into the sea.

A lifetime later Drew would type Joey's name into online search engines, press the "Find" button holding her breath. Nothing would come of it—a vaudeville smorgy of real estate agents, auto transmission mechanics, Gaelic language courses, a prep school rugby league, reunion of old university dons. Search engines, those eager mechanical butlers, invited her to spell the name differently. One result surfaced that would always trouble her—a testimonial for guitar strings, ordered from Canada. *The prices are down to earth. I can't recommend them highly enough.* Several times she would consider these few bland lines, as if her thoughts could rub them til they yielded a gleam of inference. Ultimately, she would shake her head, turn from the whiteblue light of the computer screen half relieved, half disappointed, and wander away.

IN ENVY COUNTRY

When Lena Macy went to the Ryersons' house, she always felt vaguely shamed, a supplicant. Only in their early forties, Dick and Karen Ryerson had already arrived at a station in life—let's be clear: had built that station, with luck and prescience—which seemed embarrassingly fabulous. Simply mounting the stairs to their mansion—yes, a bona fide mansion, with cement-relief fleurs-de-lis bannering each cupola—could fluster the most accomplished visitor. For the stairs angled so steeply and climbed so high—it was a mansion on a hill, of course, in a choice old neighborhood of this much-romanticized city—that one arrived at the doorbell out of breath. If you turned to look back in the ocean-chilled night, out over the tangled sloping garden— morning glories, poppies, daisies—past the quiet streets with their cold saline breezes, you saw a city spread to the bay, black velvet cloth sprinkled with chips of diamonds and pearls, long pins of sparkling points. Some tiny few of these moved along the milky sheen of water in the distance, under the moon. *Lords of all they survey*, Lena would think.

The heavy carved front door had a decorative window of leaded glass, a thin slot through which the insider might size up the outsider quicker than the reverse. Within, Patsy the fluffy toy poodle barked voicelessly, a frustrated, laryngeal sound. (Her bark—and ovaries—had been removed, Karen's promise to Dick when the animal was purchased.) When Dick and Karen expected guests they thought nothing of leaving the door un-locked (perhaps no thief would dare attempt all those stairs under the hot porchlights), and sometimes Lena would softly let herself in. A grand living room opened before her, warm and bright and perfectly empty. Magazines scattered over the koa coffee table, fireplace percolating (real or gas?—she'd never looked), thick Turkish rugs over the polished hardwood floor. Two deep sofas; two puffy armchairs piled with extra cushions, all in rich creams and autumn golds. The ceiling loomed twenty feet above, curved at its corners in the manner of early-century Victorians. It was the *scale* of things at the Ryersons' that had al-ways undone her, Lena decided. Lena came from a lifetime of small apartments and cottages, by her own admission found it hard to give up the mentality—though now, living with Phil, she was long past official grounds for it. It was more an ingrained habit, the minimalist reflex: living sparely and throwing the mass of your resources into a liquid emergency fund. *You never knew when you might have to run away*, went the secret refrain. It was so fundamental, so automatic over a lifetime of petty jobs, of renting this or that—the slogan had become nearly uncon-scious: entered her as an actual definition of being, after years of living alone with no net, as some put it. The Ryersons seemed by contrast to want to lean into large gestures: the heavy, expen-sive furniture announced intention of duration, like giant poles of a grand edifice sunk into that spot on earth. A huge oil por-trait of the couple hung above the couch, painted by someone whose name could be found on no fewer than five concurrent national magazine covers. Lena couldn't help thinking of this portrait as the culmination of the Ryerson home's theme—the centerpiece toward which visitors automatically veered, respectful of the visionary founders.

A separate dining room contained an antique oak table, rough-hewn yet of buttery and smooth surface. It ran the length of the room, with matching high-backed chairs. (Karen had bought it from a couple who'd thought they were moving—who'd then found they weren't; there'd come an interval of seller's remorse: the couple had missed the table and asked whether there might be any chance that Karen would sell it back. There hadn't.) And even though Lena hated formal dinner parties and would have broken into a sweat just to *overhear* the purchase price of much of what she gazed upon in the Ryerson home, something in her would wince as she stared at the warm, lavish appurtenances of the mansion. *Why haven't you made a comparable life*, went the hissed indictment, though in fact this never made sense. Lena had more than enough.

Lena would step into the kitchen, a lofty, airy place anchored by a red formica table, circa '50s diners, at its center. What struck most forcefully, even after years of visiting this room, was its dual function as a vast photo gallery. Everywhere you looked, photographs of every size and quality of the Ryerson clan. Karen had married Dick with two children of her own by an older fellow, an affable shipping executive, now retired. Fred had become the couple's neighbor and close friend, a virtual household member. Thus his bland, forbearing face bobbing forward like a familiar coin in the photographs. High up along the ceiling were tacked enormous blow-ups of Karen and Dick getting married in the city's famous cathedral; Karen and Dick on a Nile barque, reclining in a Venetian gondola, squinting up at the Aya Sophia. There were photos of Karen as a grinning little girl at her mother's side, her beautiful Irish mother gamely holding armfuls of younger babies. Photos of the same mother, aged but still beautiful, balancing a martini and cigarette. Photos of Karen's own two as infants sleeping, peeping from between crib bars. As toddlers picking wildflowers; sitting like train cars in the bathtub with their father. Photos of them as preteens and teens, clowning and preening. They were now starting college, suitably handsome, bright, equable, and suitably scarce. Walls and surfaces reverberated with Ryersons: at the finish lines of marathon runs, tiny beside the columns of the Paestum, perched before tall green drinks at a Deux Magots table. Some of the snaps were drugstore-booth black and whites, the sort that fed out of old-fashioned machines damp and smelling of developer: Karen with celebrity pals (she was a beloved and highly public television anchor in this city), mugging wildly at the camera, looking tan under the booth's fluorescent lights, white of their eyes too white. Lena would recall an old Steely Dan lyric: *Show business kids making movies of themselves.*

As Lena would move from wall to wall staring at these many evidences, these connect-the-dot testaments for a specific linear history brimming with apparent joy, she would feel the cumulative noise of them come to settle on her shoulders. A peculiar, antic definition of the Good Life seemed to build in the air around her, to roar in her ears the longer she stayed and stared. The flanks of photographs seemed to chorus singsong at her and by some baffling extension, to mock: *Antic life is what we do well here. Antic life is The Meaning and The Way.* Lena sometimes thought that rather than pay a formal visit to the Ryersons she would much rather just slip in while the family was out and be left alone awhile in the house with all the pictures. It would cost no social effort, no small talk, especially the kind you had no intelligent rejoinders for: Rio de Janeiro? By cruise ship? For free, because you'll be a guest speaker on board? But how delightful, how wonderful for you, she would gush while a taste of something like quinine made its way around the muscles of her face. *A museum*, she would think as she walked from one surface to the next, pausing and studying. *A shrine.*

It wasn't that Lena thought she ought to mount such a display. In fact all the billboarding seemed distastefully shrill to Lena; seemed to muddy privacy. Yet it was the sheer blatancy of all of it that seemed to force comparisons: that seemed to put her, by default, on trial. An old friend had a name for it. "Ah, we're in Envy Country now," he'd intone, smiling sadly at her. It was a condition, he'd implied, that you couldn't affect, really. You just had to pass through.

Lena had moved to this city knowing no one, and with furious energy (she was thirty then) worked her way into a slot at the city's national network affiliate station. She'd found herself recruiting guests by phone from a tiny windowless office in the station's wire-draped warren of tiny offices, for Karen's interview portion of the weekly magazine. To Lena's own amused surprise, she'd done it well. Being "no one," invisible, allowed her to take impossible risks without offending. She brought in politicians, actors, musicians; figures who were eccentric and admired; industrialists or eco-heroes or food wizards. She spoke to their managers, bringing to these "telephone safaris" (for that was how she thought of them; phoning wide to net Big Game) a distinct manner that had invented itself while she looked on. Out of her mouth warbled a voice lacking the least consciousness of any reason for hesitation. It spontaneously drew people in; they actually seemed pleased to step forward. And Karen Monahan must at some moment have noticed. For one day she asked Lena to lunch.

So much had passed since that first lunch. Lena still remembered her dread: how to dress? How to behave? She'd finally settled on the uniform that made her feel least foolish, a black cotton blazer and straight skirt; low-heeled pumps. Karen, to Lena's amazement, had worn old beige jeans, a boy's madras shirt and sneakers, her penny-colored hair pulled into a heedless stump of a ponytail—what you might wear to paint a house. Lena had wondered where they should go, confused to find herself following Karen into the cafeteria of the city hospital in the heart of old downtown, a few doors from the television station. Karen, who could easily afford a good restaurant, didn't eat much, and preferred the camouflage of the low-ceilinged, whitely-lit place. To get there you had to take an elevator, then wander along wide, polished-linoleum corridors. Occasionally a patient passed them, a distracted man or woman in wind-filled blue gown, pushing a wheeled pole on which hung fluid-filled IV bags. The two women slid trays along metallic piping, helping themselves to little mounds of carrot-jello salad and iced tea. Lena had thought at the time she should pay careful attention to this hospital cafeteria habit. It could mean something.

What do you want to do? Karen had asked as soon as they'd sat down. I mean, really want to do, she added, poking up some orange salad, eyes upon her companion curious, calm. Karen spotted, like a marksman, unmet needs in people who interested her. She liked to ride straight out to greet them—the town marshal—and set about "solving" them by connecting them with others whom she similarly wanted to "solve." It wasn't girlscoutism or matchmaking. It was, Lena thought later, more like a side-hobby to placate a mind needing motion. Get the lives to intersect and form something: a sort of human scrabble.

Radio, Lena had heard herself blurt that day under the cafeteria lights, astounded that this most secret and perhaps archaic desire of hers, never before uttered, should have been pried out in a single deft stroke, a shiny marble from a baby's fist.

I'm told I have a good voice, she added weakly, feeling her neck and face stripe with heat. I like the feel of spoken sound in my throat. I'd like to read on the air.

So you do. A lovely voice, Karen nodded, not having paused in her chewing except to sip thoughtfully from her tea straw. Karen was a thin redhead with small, keen features. She herself had a notable voice, gruff and jokey, in rather fresh opposition to her lithe figure. Karen appeared to actually like people, which seemed suspect to Lena. Too simple. Karen was smart. Why suffer foolish noise gladly? Especially when you considered that Karen was usually surrounded by self-admiring, slick media types or confused, fawning fans. Lena herself fell gratefully into time alone, her mind a washing-machine of whatever last sounds had been pouring in. They took a long time to drain off.

I know someone in the East Bay, Karen had said that day—ruminatively, as if weighing odds on a particularly obscure bet. Runs the arts department on KBNK—you remember it? The old hippie station? Very respectable now; gets national programming and funding from the Weinstein Foundation. Let me see.

And soon enough Lena had found herself driving over the bridge every week to read and host broadcasts on public radio. True, it was only part-time, but it was a beginning. She found that after overcoming initial nervousness (it had helped at first to run a few miles, unhook her bra and the top button of her pants, and drink chamomile tea beforehand)—found she loved the cozy sound studios, the padded isolated peace of them, the bluejeaned staff smiling as they nodded her cues at her through the studio glass. She loved the dove-colored light that played through the skylights of the building. Loved the feel and play of her own breath in her throat, her voice a warm, pliable liquid she could mold, speed or slow down on the air. It was soothing in the little soundbooth, softly-lit, a thickened hush around you that made the world outside seem emptied, like a retracted sea. Yet your voice was being attended by living people in a populous and noisy world, driving or cooking or cleaning. Maybe the radio sat on their office desks. Maybe they were dozing, and your voice was entering their dreams. When the clear square buttons of the phone lines sitting in front of her lit up afterward with compliments, Lena felt a slow wonder.

Maybe getting that job had had little to do with Lena's resume. Maybe it had been strictly the result of Karen's request for a favor. People were so enamored of Karen Monahan—the name and face grinning gigantically from bus-station glass and billboards along the city's busiest thoroughfares—they hailed her on the streets, lined up for her autograph or for a photo with her. Lena had always felt grateful for Karen's boost. Would she, Lena, have done the same for a near-stranger? It was hard to imagine. Lena had no *name*, no influence. Compared to Karen, it was only possible to feel like a Petitioner.

Nine years had interceded. Lena had met Phil, a man who looked like an ad for extra-hearty soup. And after a time she'd agreed to move to his pleasant suburb, where you found coffee houses and bookstores and seriously good restaurants along any block. Phil was divorced, had a house, a secure management slot in the Op-Ed department of the town's dull, sturdy daily newspaper. He had accruing retirement, few second thoughts, and unsinkable humor. The morning air in Phil's town, bordered by apple orchards, smelled to Lena like new snow. Phil himself smelled pleasantly yeasty, like rising bread dough. Lena had consented to move in. But first she'd brought Phil round to Karen and Dick's for inspection.

How anxious she'd been as they'd climbed the steps. Phil had been ahead of her, easily mounting the steep stairs. *Don't worry it to bits*, she'd scolded herself. Why the anguish? Of course she had wanted to impress Karen and Dick. She'd wanted—all right, yes. Wanted to be counted among their circle. It wasn't a motive she'd admit out loud. She'd always depicted herself a maverick. But Karen was important to her. *Never competitively*, she often told herself ferociously. *Different media*. But for contacts and—well, perhaps some of that anointedness would rub off.

Phil was aware of the fact of his going before a kind of tribunal that night, and wry about it.

Am I in appropriate garb? he had asked in his rolling baritone, glancing back and smiling down at her as they puffed that first time up the impossible climb. She'd nodded tightly in her requisite black, cologned and mascara'd and moussed. The sense of costume always mocked her. She could never quite escape the whiff of fraud about it, of being an alien in drag. Her stomach had been clenched, and she'd known that first glass of wine would go back quickly, indelicately. The two had huffed up the stairs anticipating wine: Phil because he loved to eat and drink; Lena in blind longing for obliteration of nerves.

And it occurred to her tonight, nine years later, that her stomach no longer remembered how it had knotted in the beginning. Tonight she wore jeans and a T-shirt, lazing back in her chair at the red formica table, twisting the stem of her globular wineglass with the fond, reckless confidence of repeated ritual.

The walls of photographs no longer gave her vertigo. Rarely did she flick a glance at the giant oil portrait or the buttery table. And though Lena still occasionally felt a twinge of mindfulness—awareness of a special entrée, by dint of simply being there—it had muted. Phil, of course, never gave a snort about entrée. He'd come to the friendship by affiliation: it was frosting, without power to unbalance him. He mainly wanted to see what Dick was cooking. (Dick was a deadly-serious chef and *gourmand*; both men treated every facet of food preparation with the gravity of seminarians.) Tonight the four of them sat around the formica table under the cheerful kitchen sconce with several opened bottles of excellent wine, a bowl of cashews, and seeded baguette slices slabbed with feta and kalamata olives. Patsy sniffed a steady, sharklike tour around their feet, claws clicking along the floor, stopping for intervals at her yellow dish to chew an occasional kibble. They were talking about feeling old.

The women in my office, Dick was saying, were born after Vietnam.

I'd been talking about the war, he said. And one of my assistants fixed me with this—look. Dick, she said. We weren't even *born* then. Dick raised his fair brows, looking at his company. His handsome face bore a droll, pained deadpan: ironic bafflement like Jack Benny's, an expression Lena always thought brilliant. She considered it Dick's way of slightly discounting his own startling handsomeness—he was a finely made man with a blondish buzz cut and penetrating bluegreen eyes—perhaps his way of slightly discounting all his good fortune, of knocking the chip off his good fortune's shoulder. Dick was senior partner with a law office—a nice placid one, specializing in permissions and intellectual property. He seemed to understand that while he was enjoying the fruits of a delicious confluence, he was not such a fool as not to know it was still part of the cosmic comedy: so arbitrary and momentarily revocable he should never presume to be considered its author.

Yes, oh yes, Lena was nodding. I have to face the supermarket baggers calling me *ma'am* now. And at the gym, I make sure to wear concealing things.

Ah, sweetheart, you've nothing bad to conceal, growled Phil loyally. She shot him a grateful blink. He was so sunnily *up for things*, was Phil. Sometimes she actually wished he'd just for a minute be unsteadied by fretful mental hashings, or grow dubious and stricken by some morose chain of reasoning the way she did. Instead he met each day with vigorous lists. Planned menus, fumed against the media for assorted crimes, bought flowers, rearranged the paintings on the walls. Dug up the back garden or painted the bathroom in an afternoon, soaked with sweat. Purposiveness like a booster rocket.

Karen was resting her chin against her elbow-propped hand. For me, the measure of age is the kids, of course, she said, looking thoughtful. They're dating, they're finishing school, they're hundreds of feet tall—

They're gone, Dick noted providentially, draining his glass. Phil at once applied a new bottle to it.

Karen kept her inward gaze. What they say about clichés being clichés because they are true, she went on, her eyes musing and puzzled. The whole thing truly seems to have— *streaked* by.

Karen's children were her oxygen, Lena knew. There was no subject Karen was gladder to consider, nor about which she was more irrational. It may have bored the men but Lena paid attention. Seeing it made Lena respect that Karen—so public a figure, so breezily worldly—would allow it to be seen. Karen had *willed* the coalescence of the man she wanted with the children she cherished, serenely caulking over what was still clear to Lena: that neither man nor children, of their own volitions, would have sought each others' company. But that was always true, wasn't it? Stepfather and stepkids eked a grudging coexistence with Karen at their center like a bright keystone, exactly balancing—without benefit of glue—the bricks in the archway.

The backdoor to the kitchen opened, and a tall, beautiful young man of about twenty stood before them. Patsy jumped toward him as if launched, *harf-harfing* frantically.

Grady! Karen looked up, leaned far forward like an elated child, grinning welcome at the apparition with so much shameless radiance it almost shocked Lena.

Hey, smiled the boy loosely, stooping to calm the dog. Lena could not help gaping. Karen's son by Fred (who was pleasant to regard, but unremarkable) was a model for Greek statuary. Hair sandy, eyes aquamarine, long body dense at the shoulders, heavy with careless grace. His lips were like slices of fruit; his eyes sleepy. *He lacked guile,* Lena saw with relief; would not be the sort who scanned the scene making predatory calculations. His was exactly the lazy, unassuming beauty Lena used to secretly moon over as a girl: the inadvertent Adonis. Staggering, that this splendid creature had only minutes ago been a pudgy button of a toddler, minutes later a sweaty little character who lived for snowboarding. Now Lena recalled the photo lately added to the kitchen collection: Grady ballroom-dancing with his mother. Even taller in a tuxedo, he'd looked a little embarrassed in the photo, gazing nearly straight down at Karen as they stepped together, and Karen had been lifting her face straight up to beam—ecstatically—into her son's self-conscious, sleepy one.

Hey, Grady, said Dick. He glanced up momentarily from his wine.

Dick, nodded Grady affably. Patsy, reassured, resumed her vacuuming tour. Re-introductions to Phil and Lena were made, since the last had occurred when Grady was at least three feet shorter. The boy shook hands with Phil, who angled himself toward the giant youngster as they talked. Phil did well with kids. He lived out with them a crude golden rule of his own devising: *don't be the kind of asshole you yourself would not have wanted to deal with.*

Why was the boy home?, Lena silently wondered. He was supposed to be at Brown now, wasn't he?

Have you eaten? Karen asked her son. No, answered the boy. His girlfriend was coming over; perhaps they'd get a pizza. We're having steaks, offered Karen, and at once Lena saw Dick's face twitch, and furrow. He was that moment grilling several of the finest cuts of meat money could buy in his state of the art gas-fed grill, along with other carefully plotted delicacies, on the deck just outside the kitchen. Karen insisted to Grady that some of the meat, along with some of the salad and the ke-babbed, grilled marinated vegetables, the loaf of Gruyère-garlic sourdough, the bittersweet-chocolate crème brulée, and what-ever else happened to be handy, would be available him and to Mira—who stepped in moments later, a dark, sapling-thin In-dian girl with long black hair. She smiled at the assembled, her black-nut eyes snapping with the confidence of eternal, weight-less youth.

Whatever, said Grady without inflection, soft and floppy as a plush animal. The two disappeared to do their homework.

Dick had stopped talking and his face was very dark. Karen hadn't yet seemed to notice, still flushed with the pleasure of her son's being near, like someone who'd just received an extra quart of her own blood. Phil looked sharply from one to the other, running his forefinger and thumb up and down his wine-goblet stem. Lena tried to push things back into locomotion. Someone had to make noise, at least.

Why is Grady here? she asked Karen.

Karen smiled. He hadn't liked the east. It wasn't for him. Too costly; too cold. He'd decided to try out the state university here instead. She spoke with the quick nose-wrinkle and hasty, confiding tones that telegraphed conspiratorial intimacy, in-viting you warmly into her swift logic. Of course, thought Lena. Perfectly natural to reverse a decision after moving heaven and earth to achieve it. She wondered what it had cost Karen to set up her son in an eastern apartment with tuition and books and food. Then she thought with a hot little stab of her own ridicu-lous youth: fleeing the ruthless competition of college to wait-ress and salesclerk and au pair her way around the country. But Lena had never sought help, had always worked—beholden to none. Other kids had less trouble with beholdenness, it seemed. So much, thought Lena, was determined by the luck of the draw. And Grady had drawn a mother with money.

Dick had said nothing at all, but was moving fast around the kitchen making large, banging motions, bolting an occasional gulp of wine. His face wore the same deep scowl, and Lena saw the transgression was grave. An issue, she guessed, that was sore.

Lena knew Karen would do anything for her kids. When they got arrested on weed charges, she bailed them. When they crashed cars, she found them new ones—made it seem a personal fetish of her own, shopping for cool used cars. When they dropped out of schools, she praised the intrepid adventure of the jobs they took or the travel they managed. When they re-enrolled in schools, she went with them and returned to describe, rapturously, the new campus, the neighborhood, the city, the girlfriend or boyfriend, the vehicle, the movie they saw together. Nowhere else in Karen had Lena seen a more unhesitating self-abnegation: no looking both ways before you crossed. It was motherhood pure and unalloyed. The Western world's version of a she-wolf.

It had been Karen's daughter, Adriana, a year older than Grady, who'd driven Dick mad at the beginning. In fairness, she'd been driving everyone mad equally. The girl had become intractable, a fury of destruction, almost drowning the lot of them with her. Then one day the child popped out of it for no reason. One morning Karen had wearily hollered at her daughter through the closed bedroom door that she'd be late for school.

Coming, mother, sang the dulcet voice of a stranger. The conversion had happened overnight, like an exorcism—and had stuck. The girl was now tucked happily away in a prestigious college down South. She was majoring in philosophy.

Life was full of surprises.

But tonight life was spiraling like a wounded biplane, careening nose-down, a corkscrew of thick black smoke pluming after it.

Dick turned suddenly to the group in the midst of his hapless pan-bangings and braced himself against the gas stove as if to push off. He said evenly, without looking at any of them:

Excuse me. Then he walked from the room, and in a moment they heard the massive front door open and shut, loudly. Patsy raced after the sound, *harfing* in helpless anxiety.

Karen looked blank for just a beat's fraction—then liltingly, smoothly addressed her slack-mouthed friends. Smooth as—well, as a television anchor. Phil, Lena? Would you mind taking over the steaks for a while? I'll be back very soon. Thanks so much. She said the thanks part with the silky-fake graciousness that signals finality, the tone you'd use to thank a telemarketer before hanging up on him. Karen rose, and Lena watched her take a step out of the kitchen—pausing an instant to whirl back and snatch an open, full wine bottle from among the several that stood breathing on the table. Then she padded out of the kitchen—saying No, Patsy, stay—and exited quietly by the front door.

Lena jumped to her feet without a word to Phil and ran into the living room to scramble up onto the long couch. Patsy followed, hopping at the couch edge fruitlessly. At last the dog tired of this and sat, watery eyes blinking: a thwarted echo of every human action in the house.

The couch-back abutted the living room window, which offered, like almost all the windows on the house's façade, a splendid panorama of the street below and all the way out to the bay. It was summer, and the air was shot through with the diffuse custard-rose of early evening. Lena panned left to right until she spotted Dick hiking up the steep green slope of the tiny city park a short distance opposite the house, at the top of which stood a great, old oak. Then she spotted Karen, bottle in hand, clasping its neck with a thumb over its mouth, toiling up the hill after him. She was bent forward to get a purchase on the slope. Karen must have yelled something at her husband, because Dick paused a moment to turn and see her working her way toward him. Then he turned back without expression and kept hiking. Karen double-timed it (she was thin, didn't smoke)—and caught up with him under the giant oak at the top of the little hill. There Lena watched the couple stand facing each other as their mouths moved rapidly and they made gestures. His were like an Italian chef's, though Dick was Irish by heritage. Hers were a negotiator's, sent to talk terrorists into releasing hostages. *It's always so easy to spot a fight,* Lena thought, her breath clouding the glass. So chastening. You're going along thinking of nothing, your own chores, and then you come upon a couple locked inside it: faces distorted, eyes hard and bright. A small, self-contained emergency. When you stumble onto them, Lena thought, it is like coming upon something raw and feral in the midst of organized life: a nest of baby possums in a shoe.

Dick had literally thrown up his hands. His faced looked aggrieved and severe. Karen had one hand on her slim, boy's hip. The other hand, still holding the bottle with a thumb protecting the contents, gestured back toward the house. Suddenly, abruptly as a folding chair collapsing, Dick sat down at the base of the immense tree. Karen instantly plopped herself a foot or two from him at the spreading tree base, where the ridges of roots plunged down. After a moment she handed the wine bottle to Dick. He took it, examined the label testily, lifted the bottle high to his lips and drank—just like any Tenderloin gutter-squatter. He handed it back to Karen. She drank. Neither looked at the other. Neither spoke.

Lena was enchanted.

Phil! Come look!

One sec, yelled Phil's distant, preoccupied voice, and then came the sound of the door to the back deck slamming, followed by a sizzling and a lovely smell. Patsy skittered at once out to the kitchen. The sounds and the smell were poignant to Lena as a newborn's cry. Phil had seen his duty: mastered Dick's grill and carefully harvested his buddy's spoils. The meat and vegetables could be tightly foiled in a low oven for safekeeping.

Phil came through the doorway wiping his hands with a dishtowel and kicking away the dog: a modestly pleased surgeon who'd just completed an emergency appendectomy, walking across the room with sufficiently-cleared conscience to redirect an open interest toward the next event. Phil's pace was crisp, slightly bent at the knee. It had always seemed more like a lope than a walk to Lena.

What is it? What's going on?

They're fighting, breathed Lena without taking her gaze from the window. She said it the way a small girl might have said, *a mermaid.*

Yeah? Lemme see. Why's that so nice?

Because they never fight, said Lena softly, moving over for him on the couch. They're always perfect. Her breath still made a pulsing steam on the windowglass where the tip of her nose just touched it.

You're nuts. Lemme see.

Phil brought himself to the same upright kneeling position beside her against the back of the couch, still pushing away the hysterical poodle. Patsy finally sat, watching the two adults with anxious eyes.

They saw that Dick had the bottle. His legs were splayed straight out on the ground before him in an open V, his feet tipped outward on either side. He balanced the bottle on a thigh with one arm. The other arm lay limp and useless as a hung carcass at his side. All the energy had gone out of him. His head lay its full weight back against the old tree. He appeared to be staring into distant air.

Karen sat against the tree with one knee propped up in front of her. Her body and her head, also in full weight against the tree, were turned a degree away from Dick's, and his face pointed away from hers. They looked like a custom-made salt-and-pepper set. The ones sold in Sunday magazines—that are hand painted and have titles like "Winter Morning" or "Mischievous." The title for the oak-tree situation Lena and Phil watched could possibly have been "No Dice."

And it was good for Lena to see all this. Good to know. You didn't wish ill on Karen, or on anybody, exactly. You just needed to know they ate their occasional dollop of horror. Took their turn with the floor dropping out. That they flooded once in a while with adrenalin-panic of a Hideous Mistake or arrived, screaming harshly, at Wit's End. Exactly why this should be so—

why you would need in your bones to know this—no one had yet explained. It wasn't purely because you wanted to gloat about feet of clay. That was true maybe for movie magazine types, but not the same way for this. And it was different from gossip—more than wondering what stories floated behind the golden, languid eyes of strange mansions. It was mainly, Lena began to see, that it was just damned satisfying to know Envy Country people had trouble. The kind of trouble that picked them up and shook them til they rattled: til they briefly forgot they were cute and rich and suavely in control. After that you could let down a bit, the way you might alongside a stranger after a terrifying plane flight. You could say *whew* together afterward. Not: *I beg your pardon, I don't know what the hell you are talking about.*

They're at a stalemate, Lena said. It's serious. They must be questioning the entire marriage.

But they're still drinking, Phil noted. That meant, for him, the patient had a pulse. Phil hated the way people said, The Marriage. It always sounded deadening, heavy as a steel girder. As if two people were grimacing under it, scrambling to hold it aloft, keep it from crushing them. It was why he wasn't in a hurry to marry again, though he had told Lena he was ready anytime. After nine years, you hoped you knew the worst of it.

They've never done this before, Lena said. In all our time with them.

Correction, Phil said. We've never *seen* them do it before.

This must have been the steak that broke the camel's back, Lena said.

Kids and money and food: complicated, Phil said. Should we get the boy involved?

They were still kneeling upright, watching out the window. Patsy, head on paws, stared warily.

No, Lena said after a moment. They'll work it out. Then everything will be better for a while.

How do you know that? Phil asked. How can you be sure?

The odds are for it, Lena said. She was thinking, *too much invested to throw it over. How would you begin to disassemble it. Like tearing a live woolly mammoth limb from limb.* She could see and hear the giant, stinking, hairy elephant rearing up in the Ryerson kitchen, eyes rolling back wild, trumpeting rage and terror; its fearsome giant tusks ripping through the poster of the Venice gondola as it rent open the ceiling; stumpy horned hooves crashing swaths of photographs from the walls like so many snowflakes.

She said: It can make things sweeter, having a storm clear the air.

Phil considered this. Do you wish we fought more, sweetheart?

Lena turned to him. She thought of the understructure of their dailiness—unconscious, firm, pliant—provided entirely by him. His habits had staked out the shelter they took; become signposts of a bounded safety: *hullo-hulloing* when he entered the house. Dicing garlic and onions like someone possessed first thing in the morning; racing around town and returning with crackling bags. Shaking himself into his clothes before a mirror; standing in the yard staring at his plants. Sleeping sideways in a sort of crouch, head cradled on one arm like an army grunt, as if ready to leap up and quell any crisis in a second. The sheer industry of the man; the sanguineness of his projects and plans, his robust doubling-of-the-bet with life. It had taken her up and carried her along. She wondered if she should be more superstitious about Phil's seeming physical invincibility. It was the one prayer she breathed without awareness of it, she now saw—knowing the ways of things. *Let nothing overcome him, until we are both decrepit-old. And then, O please, let it be quick, and kind.*

And was this not enviable?

Might someone this very moment be training opera glasses on her own distracted days, sighing as they craned for a better glimpse?

Phil was looking at her, solemn.

She took his face in her hands. You are the dearest man I've ever known.

They sank down to the cushions beneath them. Lena kissed him, a small series of lip-presses starting at his mouth and wandering over one cheek to the side of his neck behind his ear. Patsy raised her head and whined.

I'm very hungry, Phil said quietly after a minute.

Me, too, Lena murmured.

Pizza? he ventured.

She glanced out the window. The light was blue now, the deep rose-tinged blue of lakewater when the sun has dropped. Dick's and Karen's bodies had not moved, but their faces were aimed back toward each other. They were talking, as far as Lena could make out in the blue-rose light.

Why not pizza, Lena told him. The kids would like it. The steaks would be good for sandwiches later.

Phil hoisted himself to standing. He took her chin in his hand a moment. Then he loped off, escorted by the businesslike click-click of Patsy's claws on the hardwood, to find a phone book and a phone.

Lena turned back to keep watch.

They would wait for delivery, as long as they had to.

PICARO

Ellen has not thought about Winston for perhaps twenty years. She first knew him when she was scarcely twenty years old and he, still a child. Was the boy even seventeen when they'd become lovers? He'd probably been sixteen. Her memory of it buried in a cold, dark fog—the kind she once lived in, near Ocean Beach. Buried so long it seemed to disappear.

Until one evening not long ago, when Ellen watched a television program. A plane crash into the side of an Andean mountain fifty years before, deeply buried by the avalanche it caused, had lately risen to the surface. The glacier covering the crash had moved slowly downhill, scooping earth and ice beneath it: under, along and eventually up, wheeling, pushing its secrets up, up til they lay exposed and faintly ridiculous: found-objcts placed as if by colossal prank on the lunar-like surface of the high, snow-patched mountains. Big, deeply treaded tires bobbed into view out of nowhere, intact. An engine. And a mummified human female hand lay delicately among the rocks and snow, perfectly preserved all the way to way to mid-forearm, in ballet-like pose, graceful and stiff as a department store mannequin's.

Perhaps its owner had been resting it on the armrest of her seat when the aircraft hit the mountainside. Did they have arm-rests then? Agitated, Ellen rose from the couch, stooping in the lamplight to kiss Dan goodnight. He would stay up with the tel-evision awhile. Standing before the bathroom mirror, Ellen could see only that petrified hand, its permanent gesture of grace—though the exploring party's South American leader had waved the mummified limb disrespectfully when he picked it up, gesturing carelessly with it as if it were a drumstick he'd been eating. The hand seemed to Ellen to embody its own last moments: that its posture was blithe made its message more terrifying. She could not stop mulling the way innocent bits of people and machinery had suddenly risen to the surface, mute and harshly palpable after so long.

Then today. A typical Sunday in the gym's cardio room, where people stairclimb or cycle as they stare at reading propped before them or gaze up slack-faced at six televisions, earphones plugging their ears: Ellen is pedaling on an exercycle, reading a story in a magazine. In it, a divorced mother goes to visit a faraway friend and finds, in that friend's kitchen, her childhood sweetheart. (He is making a sandwich.) The woman secretly hopes to strike something up again with him. But his life has taken turns that have made him someone who cannot act on his old wishes.

The Andean ruins and the magazine story seem to marry in Ellen's mind, making a little explosion. She puts down the magazine, takes a drink of water, wanders to a window of the gym and leans against its frame, looking out on the tall birch trees. Their leaves shiver and ripple in the raw spring wind. She thinks immediately, and for a long time, about her last meeting with Winston.

When it happened, she had already lived many years in the world with no thought of Winston, no word of what had become of him. Ellen was thirty-five at the time. She had traveled and worked many jobs. She lived in the city alone then, caught for reasons not yet completely understood—if they ever are—in a maudlin and punishing love affair. The affair had been going on far longer than it should, longer than made any sense, and since she was an intelligent woman, Ellen despaired. She was clawing away at it every chance she got, trying to make a hole in it through which she might escape, as if the affair were a plastic bag that had sealed itself over her—a clear membrane separating her, subtly but seamlessly, from the living.

Her lover's name was Angel, which he certainly wasn't, except—Ellen had thought this during her early thrall—he was probably *intended* to be, when he was christened. Oh, intentions. And it was pronounced *On Hell*, wasn't it? He was big, dense, and dark, with a thick headdress of straight black hair. He looked like a Mayan prince. He was married and had a small son, a tiny, black-haired beauty who in Ellen's mind resembled the little boy born to Desi Arnaz and Lucille Ball. Angel's wife was a red-diaper lefty, tough and wily: she was onto him—his childlike wanderings, his serial infatuations. His wife worked Angel's guilt every possible way—staging scenes, slamming out of the house in a bitter rush, the boy mewling in her arms. Angel, torn in fine Latin torment between allegiance to his family and his belief that Ellen was the "tender heart" meant to lift him from mundane invisibility—wept easily, copiously, and could never, no matter what promises he made, leave his wife.

So Ellen and Angel saw each other, or they didn't. They took turns making vows of various sorts, and promptly broke them. When they didn't see one another for a while, Ellen felt her life starting to suck into itself, like a deflating thing. When they did, she felt as though someone might step in front of them at any moment and clap shut the hinged arm of the filmmaker's clapper, yelling "Cut!" Their encounters felt that absurdly stylized; cinematic self-consciousness seeped through their tears and embraces, as if everything they did were performed with an eye on a nearby mirror. Ellen wanted out, or believed she did. Other lives seemed to be carrying themselves along apart from this sticky, sandy web. Why couldn't she enter those other lives' midsts, shoulder in and belong to them again—unquestioned, valid, blissfully straightforward? Yet no exit seemed to appear that Ellen could yet discern. Each time she tried to end it, some invisible tether caught her and yanked her severely back, and each time it did she felt she was going mad—trapped in an elaborate Borgesian punishment, pressing along the walls of a lightless room, feeling blindly for the seams of a door, the air supply running out. Ellen kept creeping: edging her fingertips on.

But sometimes she'd have to sit down and cry.

The phone call arrived, she remembers, one dark, foggy evening.

"Hey, Ellen-Jellen. Hey, Jelly *Bean*." Though it had been fifteen years, she knew it was Winston Rattle. Jelly Bean had been his nickname for her—a strange skewing of her name that he'd once thought a clever tease. It had always bothered her—it was artless and affectionless—but she'd felt back then (she was scarcely twenty; he, sixteen) she had to accept it because it was his only expression of anything like intimacy, though it had also had the dismaying effect of distancing and mocking her. It even seemed, unhappily, to strip her of her sex. Which was odd, since sex had been a major activity for them, as she recalled.

Winston's voice hadn't changed, though it had filled out and sagged a bit, like a middle-aged man's body. It was still slow and rough; suspicious and cautious, Bogarty. She remembered at once how she had diagnosed this manner: it had been his self-protection, she'd thought, this tough and skeptical sound. His voice woke her memory the way smell or old music does, setting off a chain of associations: how she had resolved as a girl, in Earth Mother mode, to melt Winston's tough Bogie front by cosseting him. She would be the good medicine, the Love Antidote. She'd set out to show him she was rare and true: tough wasn't necessary. He'd never dropped the mode, though, apparently. Not even now.

"Winston Rattle. What are you doing here?" She was surprised at her own aplomb. Maybe it was because she was currently steeped in such relational gore—her history with Winston seemed a picked pimple by comparison.

"I'm here because I'm on business, Jelly Bean," he answered in that falsely hearty, have-I-got-a-deal-for-you tone. "I'm on a mission." Winston had found work as an entomologist's assistant when she'd last seen him, and it seemed he still did something like that now—traveling to capture and classify the insect life of Missouri, where he now lived. It had used to be Northern California, and he'd called her from towns like Willits, from rooms in roadside motels whose grainy televisions he'd be watching from the requisite lumpy beds, eating shitty, greasy food. Winston's complexion had been a mystery ride, she suddenly remembered, sometimes pinkly boyish and smooth, sometimes erupting uglily. Well, he'd been a kid, hadn't he.

"I'd like to see you, Jelly Bean," he added in that half-cautious, half-swaggering growl. Protecting itself, always hooded in case of rejection. She listened, and remembered the way Winston kissed. A particular feminine abandon in it. As if he allowed himself to go into a swoon; something innocent and receiving, even corruptible about his soft, slightly parted lips. Winston's body had resembled that of Michelango's *David*, Ellen recalled. She'd even tried sketching him once or twice, reclining nude and pale and smooth in her bed—his youthful proportions, dark curls—a relaxed, natural beauty of the sort older men turned to watch. Even then, as a naïve girl, she had seen that Winston carried his beauty with a careless but distinct awareness of it. Without any outward sign he was mindful of people's admiration the way a beautiful young girl might be: accepting silent homage to something he'd been vested with.

Part of Ellen, at the moment of his call, did wish very much to be distracted. Even better, admired. Admired without complication. Winston now lived far from her, and had a life out there. He'd mentioned a girlfriend; some muffled sort of difficulty with her. A tiny *ping* at the way-back of Ellen's mind pushed experimentally at the idea, small as silver b-b shot, of striking something up with him. She could hear behind Winston's words the same idea, a pituitary pellet. She didn't like this presumption, in herself or him—it felt coarse—but found she could not dismiss it out of hand. She agreed to dinner. A Spanish place, Picaro, down the avenues, nearer to the ocean. She wouldn't let him come to her apartment. It was too full of the rawness of her present life—and she had at least to protect the privacy of her street address (making a mental note to get her phone number changed to an unlisted one). There had to be *some*thing between her and god knew who-all, pushing at the cave door of her ragged-ass existence.

In Winston's voice she heard the clear gleam of interest. It was archeological play, she sensed, an adventure dig. She did not cancel the notion in her own thoughts, but kept it tucked up under them somewhere, a coin under a pillow.

It was at that interval a "not-seeing" time in the Angel/Ellen wars. He had gone back to his wife yet again, whimpering. Ellen had tried to kick him in the stomach just before he did. They were parked a block away from his wife's flat. Ellen had understood, with or without words, that he'd returned to his wife, eaten food there, fucked his wife again for the billionth time, slept with her. For some reason this homeyness (as she imagined it) set fire to Ellen: the shiny fortress of it, the screwed-tight coziness taunted her, cutting her with swift little slices second by second, leaving her dazed with rage. Once Ellen had chased Angel down the street, maddened, barefoot, wearing nothing but a thin cotton kimono. Angel had run very fast. She had run barefoot on the cool gritty sidewalk until her lungs seared her, until she'd had to stop in the silent warm night, the deserted sidewalk, the forsaken, blank street, hands on her knees, heaving air and sobs.

This time, in the car, Ellen had tried to kick him—she was behind the wheel, he at the other side of the front seat—but he'd seen her foot shooting out karate-style, and flattened his midsection against the car door behind him, scooting backward quickly so that it prevented her from placing the kick squarely enough to do any damage. And this bungled blow would continue to frustrate her in recollection, against all accrued reason, for years. Whenever she re-summoned the scene, she could still taste her desire to hurt him (that gray, cold day), feel her foot connecting in one hard, deep slam to his soft midsection. Hear his breath shoved out. See him fall out the door onto the street, on his back. But Angel was a nimble fellow. He'd learned to be.

In fact Angel had small, twitching eyes and a feral wariness about him like a rabbit's. Years of scampering at the rough edge of white men's laws had polished him smooth, made him know how to move without attracting the wrong kind of attention. What currents to sniff, when to dash, when to recede. Angel was most at ease, Ellen knew, in the type of bar where she'd first met him—jazz bars full of smoke and sticky uriney beer smells, movement and sound into which he could slip invisibly, take a quiet seat, nurse a beer. Eventually he'd strike up talk with anyone at hand, about anything at all. Angel needed response—anyone's—to feel he was alive. She wouldn't understand this completely for a long time. It had been she who'd been at hand to respond, of course, arriving at the bar that fateful first night to hear a trumpeter she liked—she who'd come alone; self-conscious, brave, ignorant. She'd noticed Angel, been drawn to his Chief Broom looks, laughed at his clumsy jokes.

They had talked. She had driven him home. Home where his wife and son slept, waiting for their *Papi*.

She'd been single and lonely so many years, she didn't know how to know better.

It makes a queer backwash when someone from one life you are leading slaps up against someone from a different, earlier life. Each seems to challenge the other's physical existence, like pieces of furniture brought together from different planets. Or bringing your second-grade teacher, her thick ankles drooping over her sturdy nurse's shoes under long, billowy, Amish-length skirts, into the room to meet your current lover in his T-shirt and leather jacket. "Mrs. Mahoney, this is Angel Gutierrez. Angel, this is Mrs. Mahoney. Mrs. Mahoney, Angel is a machinist for a candy factory. Angel, Mrs. Mahoney pinned my penmanship up on the class bulletin board."

Ellen agreed to have dinner with Winston one week from the night of his call. But during that week, something queer happened.

Nausea.

Waves of it. At first a whispering unease, then more emphatic, a sudden deep rolling twist—enough to make her stop walking or reaching or whatever she might be doing when it hit. At the same time she began to comprehend, slowly and stupidly, that no period had shown yet that month. At approximately the same time came the onset of sharp, highly specific longings for pancakes and rotisserie chicken, for donuts with peanut butter on them and chocolate milk, for patty melts and cottage cheese and Egg McMuffins. But when she'd drive out of her way to get these things into her mouth they tasted metallic, as if infused with powdered iron or rust.

The food tasted like blood.

She took a morning off from her job and walked up the hill to the neighboring university clinic for the test, her heart fibrillating shallowly. Hope was a dulled, witless thing, because it knew it was not admissible this time. She watched the wine-colored syrup pop cheerfully from beneath the tender inseam of her open arm through the translucent plastic tubing, colorful burgundy display looping-the-loop into the clear-glass beaker.

The call came three days later. The voice on the other end of the phone a woman's, youngish, deliberate and steady. That voice had practiced delivering its payload to every manner of response. How must it feel, Ellen wondered, to have people wait on your words this way. The way they might stand in a Coliseum's dirt arena, amid the animal dung and the white-noise roar, attending a Roman ruler's whim.

Positive. Four weeks.

Oh, Christ oh Christ oh Christ.

The restaurant meant to be a gothic affair. It was stony and chilly, dungeon dark. Fat candles sat on ornate black iron sconces nailed into the walls. Waiters moved about, wearing the familiar waiting person's expression of fixed, grim aversion. The Gypsy Kings played on the speaker system—music that always made Ellen think of being sold into Moroccan slavery. Their furious guitars, their wails ululating like mosque prayers, their forlorn urgency—made you want to misbehave. Drink liquor straight from the bottle, pitch your half-smoked cigarette aside impatiently, slap someone. Ellen would come to hate the music. It seemed to stand for everything she had thought she loved, in the beginning, about Angel. And it was dawning now that Angel's tremulous urgency was the most tedious possible groove to get stuck in. The whole business had even begun to border on comic, to seem outsized and floppy—an outsized Musketeers hat, ostrich-feather falling down over some kid's face.

It was hard to think of a Gypsy King standing around with a limp garden hose, watering the grass. Or pushing a cart down a fluorescent supermarket aisle, eyeing the canned corn.

Or leaving his perfectly capable wife and innocent child to marry his pregnant girlfriend.

Winston was waiting for her at a small table. She spotted him at once, from the back. Same color hair. Same back. It squeezed her in her chest for an instant. Winston was balding. In his thirties.

Ellen had parked two blocks from the restaurant because she had needed time to clarify, to gather nerve and wits. She wore a black sweater, black skirt. What did she tell herself in those few minutes? What do any of us tell ourselves? Something on the order of *must go forward*. The late afternoon was typical near the beach, where the streets snub out and the trolley tracks become a circular cul-de-sac. The end of the line. Thick, gray fog bore down like packed batting, almost mist, finest droplets vibrating as they hung, beading. You could scarcely see. The heavy fog seemed to pet her as she moved through it; cool and wet, cobwebbing everything the same gunmetal gray.

Winston turned quickly as she approached from behind, as if his peripheral vision were so tautly strung it could apprehend the least motion. He eyed her in one practiced sweep as he half-rose; Ellen flinched.

"Hey, Jelly *Bean*." Winston grinned tightly. He did not move to take her hand or embrace her. His eyes shone sideways at her a little wildly, forehead and cheeks radiating a faint pink, as if he were alarmed at being caught out at something. Ellen remembered this look.

"Winston," she said, leaning quickly to peck his cheek. It smelled of men's cologne. He wore dark pants and a Pendleton shirt. The boy had turned into a middle-aged version of his boyhood self. Though in truth he would have been about thirty-one that day, in appearance at least he'd gone from seventeen to forty-five somehow. With what between?

She sat. Her stomach rippled. A parachute, lifting and settling slowly, blorpy and bubbling.

"How are you, Jelly Bean?" he said in a tone that seemed to spread itself across the table like a fanned-out line of cards. She wished to God she had not agreed to this, and silently added it to the long, long list of Never Agains.

"Not so well as I wish, Winston," she answered. Her glance bounced around the dim room. The music, the hollow, musty smell of the wax and fake stone walls, the deathless howls of the Gypsy Kings, were making her feel a bit faint.

"Strange stuff has happened since you called."

"What sort of stuff?" He was on it at once, the new note in her tone, different from last week's on the phone, and alertness prickled over his face. Winston's features were actually pert; nose smallish, black-brown eyes watchful. It was his hairline that had most changed, clipped short and shrinking perceptibly backward like an atrophying lawn; it must have caused him grief. Ellen was truthfully sorry. It wasn't fair, of course: men were bequeathed hair or bequeathed its absence, a random gene toss, coalescing atoms. Nobody deserved grief for that. Ellen remembered Winston's father's bald head, and wished, as she often did, that she could realign these things. She would fix it permanently so no one cared about the way their nose bumped or their eyebrows joined or their thighs strained at the seams of their jeans. She would fix it so we all moved about happy and loose, sleek and iridescent and unisexual as guppies. We'd all be translucent. Able to see each other's guts, the absolute same as anyone else's. Heart, liver, stomach, intestines. Little traveling, lighted displays of neatly packed organs.

She didn't have it in her to lead Winston down a falsely busy path. She'd never been able to avoid answering a direct question directly.

"I'm pregnant, actually, Winston," Ellen heard her mouth speak the words. She waited, dull and queasy, watching him. Winston's features emptied and his eyes grew mottled, though they were still trained on her. The information was glancing off him without real penetration, she saw; it was more than he could take on, or in.

Some sort of behavioral statute of limitations applying here, Ellen thought. She may as well have told him she'd contracted polio.

"Is it—" he paused carefully. Precarious, this. "Someone who wants to have it with you?"

"No. Not exactly," she said.

"No," she corrected. "It's a mess. He is married." How could she possibly describe the hemorrhage of emotion and sex and earnestness that was Angel?

"Jelly Bean," he said. "What're you gonna do?" This was not spoken compassionately, but with a survivalist's curiosity—the way one truant schoolkid might ask another how he planned to evade the police.

"I don't know, Winston." She looked at the tablecloth, a field of whiteness. Against it, her mind fanned successive images of the ludicrous, petitioning Angel. She had phoned him the previous Saturday morning, driven all the way out to the factory in South City where he labored. Met him in the parking lot, confronted him. The eucalyptus trees fencing the area nodded, waving their long loose leaves in the cool morning wind off the sea: seemed to embank the two in the bottom of a big bowl. Angel had wept, of course. Fallen to his knees and embraced her, pushing his face into her belly. He'd taken both her hands and kissed their fingertips and palms. He begged her to have the baby by herself. Ellen worked in an office as a secretary. Her parents were dead. She had no savings. But—a gust of inspiration—he'd send her money! He had a friend who'd done it, he told her. (*Let's be clear*, Ellen thought, *his wife had this friend*.) Carried it all off alone. Gone to the hospital, expelled the infant, came home unescorted on the city bus clasping the infinitely small, infinitely helpless new creature—a creature which would, in about five minutes, Ellen knew, turn into a hulking, hungry, despising teenager who'd demand money. But that first vision of the pale, exhausted woman seated on the city bus, looking out the window into the cottony haze of day, her tiny issue the size of a loaf of bread wedged in her arms—made Ellen go cold. Imagine a baby wailing in her apartment, while a few blocks away Angel was tucked in sweetly with wife and *mijito*. Imagine Angel pressed to the cyclone fence outside the preschool, tears streaming, or knocking on Ellen's door at all hours, drunk, plying the bewildered child with weepy injunctions and symbolic little trinkets under the pretext of Mysterious Uncle. And that would only be the beginning. The beginning.

The waiter, a man of about forty, had glided noiselessly to the table's edge and stood inquiringly, managing to partly cloak the bitter fatigue and disdain contorting his expression. So many of these men were gay, their natural looks starting to evanesce, fine sheen of kitchen-steam perspiration covering their brows, and Ellen knew waiters were not generally offered health plans. What on earth was to become of them?

But why limit the question to waiters?

"Well, hey now." Winston was still looking at her, trying to gauge what might be recoverable here. "Let's eat something, Jelly Bean."

"Winston, could you please, please, *please* stop calling me that," she said, in a voice that came out thin and frayed.

He colored up promptly as a stoplight.

"What looks good?" He seized one of the long, laminated menus and fixed his gaze furiously on the columns of words.

Ellen tried to rouse herself to the ivory-colored cardboard whose lettering was like old-fashioned hymn music. Paella was supposed to be good here. She gave up and asked Winston to pick anything for her. The place was not cheap, but she'd not thought of that earlier. She'd only been hoping, when she'd suggested it, to—what. Provide a setting.

Winston ordered the dinners and asked for wine; when it came he tilted his glass briefly toward her and bolted a fortifying gulp. She took a polite sip. The food arrived, a vast ceramic oval platter of blackish things and whitish things. Her stomach dimpled a little; hungry but uneasy. She touched the food with a fork, prodding it gently as if it might move.

"Winston, I'm not feeling awfully good. I think I might have to go home soon."

"Aw, Jel—aw, c'mon now, kid. It's been so many years! How often does a chance like this—" He amended himself. "—a reunion like this happen?" He smiled in a lopsided way, adding as if in bright afterthought:

"I'd like to see your apartment."

He was peering at her.

She stared at him. A voice hissed: *fill the time, fill the time.*

"Winston, what's your life like? Are you happy?" She licked some beans from the tip of her fork. They tasted good at first; in the next beat a coppery dog food flavor tinged the insides of her cheeks.

The question annoyed him. Too dry and high-minded, she guessed, like public television compared with porn.

He shrugged, chewing. "I don't know. I'm all right. The town's okay, boring as hell. The job's good. Girlfriend's kind of a roller coaster, though."

Why?

"Wants to live together, get married." He grimaced and again colored a little. "The usual."

Ellen always felt stung by reports like these, implicated by them. Home and family appeared the only things, time and again, that her sex seemed to publicly desire. It shamed her that it seemed true for herself as well—those two things a sort of primal recourse. Everything else—travel, school, jobs—slid witlessly as soap in and out of one's grasp, despite best plans. And even though the year was already 1985, the big proverbial butterfly net was still—still!—what men joked about and shied nervously away from, clattering off like cartoon characters in every direction. Princess or peasant, the sorry lot of women still trapped in that dreary reflex: to merge and file toward the distance, two by two.

"Winter sucks," Winston was declaring, with a knowing leer. Again she was struck how he still barked these ugly sounding words as a kind of shield, as if to seal the least crack of vulnerability. It was easy to see how her misty girlhood self might have resolved to overcome this. Wendy to all Lost Boys.

He brightened. "Hey, Jel. Remember the days when all we did was hang out and smoke dope? Remember Spring Run?"

Oh yes, she remembered. College. Most of her gang, dropouts still working for the university. In spring all the men arriving in early morning on thundering black Harleys, blackly shining and snorting like barely tamed bulls; the men too in black, leathered and helmeted, the women cleaving to them on the rear of the seat or driving Volkswagen vans. Down Highway 1 to Big Sur they all rumbled; campsites were assembled, pup tents and little geodesic shelters by the cold crashing sea—how cold it was, but in those days you didn't mind getting cold and wet and sandy, everything damp and salty and reeking of campfire and weed smoke—the wine, the beer, the barbecue, the grass laced with PCP, the mescaline. They played guitars, sang.

How had they survived? Everyone working the strangest jobs: obscure, patchy things. Washing beakers, canning peaches, nude dancing, library filing. Catching bugs in jars for the state. Grace, sheerly, was how they'd survived. A grace they'd embodied—none of them would for one millisecond question it. War was far away: the boys showed up at the draft board in drag (everyone helped dress them in lace and hose), or went to Canada. Pain was what you felt in love. They all crammed into someone's old car together, backfiring down the highway to the drive-in where they watched *Peter Pan* loaded up on PCP. Ellen remembered watching the cartoon's children, Wendy, Michael and John, fly off with Peter and Tinkerbell into the glittering indigo night—the song's chorus following the children like a glitter-trail. *You can fly, you can fly, you can fly.* How it had squeezed her heart, an anguish of longing for the children to be safe, for them never to come to harm. For goodness to prevail. She remembered crying out words that must have escaped the car window into the far-starred, hay-smelling night: "How dear! How dear!" It had never occurred to Ellen until this minute that that loopy era, of Wendys and Lost Boys and all their sweet foolishness, might have outright used up her grace quota for life.

"Of course I remember, Winston. Do you miss that time?"

"I had my head up my ass—but there were some fun times, weren't there."

"We were all that way then, Winston. It was automatic, a factory feature."

They talked about what had become of people in their old gang, though neither of them had much information. People disappeared, and with them, stories to tell. Ellen hadn't thought for years about her days of living with Winston. As they talked it came back in patches, a screen filling in by pixel-sized bits. An actual little wooden cabin near the railroad side of town: when a train passed (its lovely, mournful whistle) the crockery on the kitchen shelves really did shake. She'd loved that cabin, until, until—but when, exactly, had she ceased to love it? She'd worked hard to cook like Winston's Italian mother, making minestrone and lemon meringue pies and bagels and English muffins and pot roasts. He'd devoured it all. The food would be gone, and then so would he, and then the cleaning would remain. But it wasn't that. There was something else—something had happened. Ellen pressed her mind to locate the ache of unease. Suddenly enough she found it.

The bed. The made bed.

A distant girlfriend had visited Ellen one day in the middle of the week, a girl from out of town. Ellen had no remnant left in mind of the girl's name or history, or even how they'd been acquainted. But she remembered her face: mild, cheerful, freckles. Bobbed sandy hair. Tomboyish, athletic. The girl must have stayed overnight on the living room couch. Ellen recalls, fainter than a picture from a baby book, the pleasant conversation between the three of them at dinner. The following day Ellen left for work. At the time, Winston had no job except high school, and it was summer. That day the girl was to have returned to her town, but the girl and Winston would have had part of the day together. Ellen had come home from her library job in the afternoon and found the bed, the bed she and Winston slept in, carefully made up in a foreign way. She remembers standing there, staring at the bed.

She saw it again clearly: the crisp, smoothed cotton madras spread, the careful little tuck where it folded under the neatly aligned pillows. A hotel-made bed, a way she never made a bed, and Winston had never bothered to make a bed in his life. Coming home to that tidy bed had been for Ellen like finding the house violently burgled: every drawer yanked and dumped, closets gutted; furniture overturned and glass smashed.

Ellen was just a girl herself then.

As she sat transfixed, gazing at the recalled scene, the lens on it seemed to dilate very wide, to envelop her and Winston sitting fifteen years later at the table in Picaro, and then to pan back: her head bent, dabbling slowly at her food, staring into the white tablecloth. Winston eating and drinking with big, American gestures, watching her with a monitoring attention: attention waiting for the signal it sought.

The oldest attention in the world.

This time the voice that had urged *fill the time*, spoke quietly.

A cad then, a cad now.

She blinked. Just because a chunk of time passed did not guarantee that somebody grew smarter, or better. Just because a seventeen-year-old was perpetuated along by food and drink and oxygen into his own future, into the body of a middle-aged man with a social security number and an address—didn't translate as some sort of automatic redemption.

Wherever had she gained the idea that it could?

Ellen's stomach bunched up wickedly. The cramp of nausea and hunger woke her to her present, and her predicament: O how far, but how unrewardingly far, from the early years! Stupid adulthood, brought to you directly by stupid youth. She fell gloomily silent. Did a life amount then only to this? A series of unconnectable neighborhoods, each with its resident, motley cast? Its roving brats, its garbage collection, its weedy parking lots and barking dogs?

Winston, still eating, was alert, watching her.

"What are you going to do tonight?" he finally asked.

"I'm going to try to sleep, Winston."

"Aw, Jel. It's early still. Why don't you show me your apartment? We can have another drink there, right? Howzabout it?"

Again he smiled in that lopsided way, cocking his head—his best rendition, she knew, of Beguiling. Poor goddamn Winston!

Hoping he could infect her with his *what the hell* itch, just by bearing down on it with all his will. Hoping she'd somehow snap like a pop bead into the mindset, take him up on it. She had after all, she knew, sounded amenable on the phone. But that was before she'd received her rude news. A lousy script for a painfully unfunny movie, and now she had stumbled—nauseated, facing Winston's shameless eagerness over cold, gelatinous food—on this crowning touch.

But more would be required. In the doctor's office, up on the paper-covered table, legs apart, dreamy on valium, listening in wonder to the bubbling vacuuming machine, holding the kind doctor's hand. She'd be praying then, for forgiveness. For whatever grace the cosmos might still see its way clear to accord her.

"Now, Ellen, after this you must try harder not to get yourself knocked up," he would smile sadly when it was over, squeezing her hand. There would be no pain. He was a gentle man who was close to retiring; gallantly, he'd use the vernacular in sincere effort to ease her. A girlfriend would wait in the lobby to drive her back. Maybe they could get some breakfast on the way.

Maybe it would taste good.

She forced herself to focus her eyes on the wary Winston across the table.

"Winston, I can't. I'm sorry. I can't do that," she said.

His smile faded. She began to talk very fast.

"In fact I really have to go now. Thank you for dinner—thank you for coming—here's some money, okay? No, really," she added quickly as she rose, pushing the bills under his hand when he opened his mouth, stopping his voice. "No, really. Please."

"And thank you, Winston. Really. It was great seeing you."

He was standing. She pecked him again—his face quickly turning toward hers, eyes closing, lips opening softly in reflex—and she fled.

She walked back to the car in the cooling mist. She would drive the few blocks to Ocean Beach. Walk a long, cold, sandy walk. Look out to the fogged edge of the gray, white-chopped sea: the far edge where she believed her own destiny dwelt, a not-yet-born thing. She would drive there singing the song, the anthem that had filtered up from the clumsy, innocent deeps of those years ago. If her eyes spilled while she drove, no one would see. *You can fly, you can fly, you can fly.*

Ellen turns from the gym window, the view of the shimmering birch branches beyond it, with a sigh. Time to clean up. There is the Sunday paper to collect, the bread for sandwiches, the olives. Dan will be waiting, probably fooling with the irises

out front—he always looks so severe, Churchill at Yalta, studying his bushes and blooms as if they were about to speak back
to him, whacking away branches and weeds, his face too sunburnt, his silver hair flashing in the sun. Their granddaughter
will stop by soon—Dan's son's toddler Bethany, a honey-haired
child who races to the books Ellen keeps for her, to be read over
and over. The little girl's exhausting, but Ellen loves her smell—
of baby lotion—and her willingness, at scarcely two, to musi-
cally recite any word Ellen may utter. Another baby is due
momentarily now, a brother, they think, for Bethie. You can tell,
they say, by the heartbeat.

The noon light is powdery; she and Dan might just have
time for a short walk.

Destiny wore such mild clothing.

It might have been otherwise.

You could summarize in sentences.

You could say she went on living alone. That the Angel
habit, and some others besides, finally shrank away: rolled out
to the horizon and off its edge, like a dwindling ball of lightning.
That she lived awhile, had dinner somewhere, met a man, had
more dinner, lived with him, fought him, reconciled and—for
a thousand ineffable reasons—stayed on. But that wouldn't
begin to explain the whole of it. The whole now appears to be
something more like the long view of time itself: a series of infinitesimal accretions and losses. Years of them churning and
melding, yielding up at last a smooth, habitable surface: a living
present on which she might comfortably stand. The time for
glaciers is not yet at hand. Technically, of course, they can loom
up anytime. We know that.

But they won't come just yet.

And that is all one might reasonably ask.

SANDY CANDY

Doriben's a resort town on the eastern coast of Spain. You could suggest it's like Miami Beach, with its aging neo-natives, flaccid in shorts and aloha shirts, mixed in with Cubans of all walks, hungry for work and a better life. Or maybe like Reno, Nevada in August, when everything's glinting with heat, and people who live for miles in any direction, pale or leathery, fat or thin, with blank, addled faces—creep in to wander the neon streets. Not exactly what you'd first expect of Spain.

Yet Doriben was where Lorna found herself one summer, with her husband, Brad. They had scooted south by train, to what is optimistically called the white coast (it is more a dirty brown), in an effort to find sun after a cold and raining France, and to afford several more weeks in Europe than they might otherwise have, before heading home to jobs and chores so deeply ingrained that both could replay them anytime in detail in their minds—the precise heft and sheen of every pen, every stained coffee cup, even the motes floating in tired light from their office windows.

Brad owned a sizeable hardware store, and Lorna was assistant to the vice-president of a dried fruit company, both in the pretty orchard town of Sebastopol, California. It was blissful to be on their own, for a time. Brad had a stepson by an earlier marriage who'd had a couple of babies, so though Lorna and Brad were only in their forties and had no children together, they were grandparents by default. Lorna had three nephews, Brad a widowed mother. He had obligations to his staff, Lorna to her colleagues' birthdays and weddings and pregnancies: a sticky web of relational duty enmeshed them the instant they were home. Lorna sometimes told Brad she felt they were not so much a marriage as a clearing house.

Lorna and Brad knew only that Doriben was inexpensive, and that for this reason British working class folk, many on the dole, came to the town in droves on cheap charter flights and buses, to 'ave their 'olidays, as they pronounced it. The couple found a hotel, clean and comfortable, a simple square hive of five or six stories. Their room had a smidgen view, between skyscrapers, of the sea beyond and the hotel pool below, and it had a good bathroom, which made Lorna clap her hands. Brad had done the figuring, and found they could stay at least two or three weeks in Doriben without harming what remained of their travel funds. As they wandered the town it appeared that a gigantic duffel-sack had been opened and shaken upside down, dumping every component of blue-collar British life onto an arid section of Spanish coast. Rows of shanty-cafés lined the streets like mail slots, their scribbled blackboard menus offering winter meals: bangers and mash, fish and chips, greasy breakfasts, drinks at all hours: bar after bar named things like The Dog's Bollux, fairly giving away liquor and beer. Kids were proclaimed to be welcome everywhere, and often shot pool while the adults got drunk.

These bars and cafés were filled with a population that saw the sun so little during their working lives, their bodies and faces had mustered a thick protective layer like a callous: ruddy and scored and tough, sometimes blubbery. The young people were of a paleness close to blue. All smoked without ceasing. They drank daylong, lolling in the sun like huge sea lions, occasionally shoving each other into the icy pool, shouting and screaming, crawling back out to drink and sun more. They coated themselves with oil and lay heavy and vacated, like they'd temporarily died. The older women sunned bare breasted. The hotel's loudspeakers shrieked the same Rolling Stones album every day, so that Brad and Lorna learned to wake to the "woo-woo" chorus from "Sympathy for the Devil." The Spanish, whose economy was struggling back from the Franco years, had learned every particular of their British guests' desires. Ice cream and candy, miniature golf, soda, cigarettes, cheap beer and liquor, old rock music at top volume, tabloid newspapers and karaoke. If you circled the town from the air it might resemble a futuristic coliseum on the sea, with skyscraping hotels forming its walls and a spreading flea market its floor: streets flanked with barracks of worthless goods propped in neat rows: dolls, radios, plastic toys, watches, shoes, sexual novelties.

At night the town became a reckless midway, and in the beginning to Lorna it seemed at least festive, like a tawdry county fair. She watched families and couples walking the streets or sitting in the giant pubs, smoking and drinking and nattering loudly. The kids were boisterous and small-eyed—they stared slack-mouthed at Lorna across the smeared pub tables—but they seemed to want to be where they were. Glossed-up younger couples wandered the nighttime streets; packs of teenaged girls stalked on spike heels, in tube dresses spangled with glitter. The girls left a trail of rank perfume, shooting guilty, excited glances at people they passed.

Lorna and Brad walked, and watched.

The whole town's a sideshow, Brad said, running a hand through his hair.

So it seems, said Lorna. She kept her arm firmly in his.

But no one menaced them, and in fact they could finally afford to relax in one place for a while. Lorna exulted to be able to put her shirts and shorts in the drawers of the hotel room, to have naps, hours in which to read the heavy hardback novel she'd lugged. Brad discovered where the single copy of the *International Herald Tribune* was sold and loped there happily every morning. The two drank their coffee looking out to a choppy blue sea, past the boardwalk strung with lights.

Brad was a friendly man by nature; it was one reason he excelled at his work. People trusted him; kids liked him; animals rubbed at his legs. Soon enough he announced to Lorna he'd met a nice couple in the downstairs sports bar watching soccer matches. Erleen was a retired nurse, Stan a retired soccer coach: Liverpudlians both, chatty and game for any distraction. They'd invited Lorna and Brad to "do Doriben" with them that evening. They knew, they said, where the cheapest pints were, and the cheapest dinners, and all the entertainment that mattered.

Lorna had a sinking feeling about it, a feeling she often got when Brad struck up another acquaintance. It meant losing their privacy—what remained of it. It meant presenting, inquiring. The volleyed gabble of trading background information. She shoveled it forth all year, at her own job and for Brad's staff, rounds of family, friends. At home she found herself punching the erase button for each message in their answering machine as if killing scurrying roaches. Brad was a dear man, but a sort of roving, happy dog: eager for liveliness and petting. He craved others to talk to in the course of their travels. This didn't offend her, or rather, she worked to keep it from offending her. Their natures were antithetical this way; over years they'd contrived to live around it, and she had resolved this trip to try to show him more appreciation.

The four met at Churchill's, where two tall pints cost fifty cents. Erleen and Stan looked their parts—looked a good ten years older than their actual ages, which were close to Lorna's and Brad's—their skin like jerked beef, dark and creased from cold and from direct, baking sun during the few weeks each year they could escape the cold. Their beer went down in rapid, systematic draughts; Lorna saw at once she couldn't hope to keep up. She gave her undrunk glass to Brad.

The hot sun dipped behind a skyscraper, turning the late afternoon to brass.

We're taking you to Sandy Candy tonight, Erleen was saying. You can't say you've seen Doriben until you've seen Sandy Candy. Absolutely not.

What, or who, was Sandy Candy?

It has to be seen to be believed, Erleen said, leaning forward, her face a mass of grinning creases. Erleen's hair was cut short like a man's.

We can't say more, she said, glancing at her husband.

Stan laughed and shook his head. You have to see it to believe it, he repeated. Stan was missing a tooth to the right of his incisors. He had an affable smile anyway. He wore a silver chain, combed his sparse hair back with cream, puffed constantly at a cigarette. Erleen, too, kept a lit ciggy, as she called it, traveling fast between her fingers and lips. She'd been told she should stop; as a nurse she had watched people die of emphysema. She shrugged, smiling. When she laughed it became a cough, a great phlegmy threshing deep in her chest.

The four sat outside in the coppery light. Brad kept an eye on the rugby game on the TV hung outside the bar. Three more televisions hung inside, tuned to the same game. Rugby looked rougher than anything Lorna had seen before. The men shoved each other into the mud, bleeding, trampling each other like starved animals over a bit of food. People at the other tables shouted at the screen.

Let's start out showing you all the cheapest bars, Erleen said when their glasses were empty.

They walked from den to den, each with its ear-splitting sound system. One was filled with old people singing along with a miked pianist. Everyone had beers before them, swaying in unison at their tables and benches. Let Me Call You Sweetheart, It's a Long Way to Tipperary. Erleen and Stan swayed and sang on their bar stools, grinning into each other's eyes. They insisted on going behind the bar and making Brad snap their photo with their arms around the bartender, a woman with a messy ponytail and cigarette at her lips. The bartender's face grimaced for the camera, accustomed to the ritual. There seemed no law in Doriben against bartenders drinking on the job. In the swaying and singing and clouds of smoke, Lorna and Brad smiled at each other. It would make one hell of a story.

Lorna had ceased trying to keep up with the others' drinking (even Brad, who loved pints, was having trouble), and sipped soda. Both she and Brad were red-eyed with the smoke, and Lorna would have given a lot to go back to their room, bathe the stench from her, read, sleep. But the evening had only begun. Erleen and Stan steered them past ragtag groups of revellers, past barkers in the doors of lounge acts (the barkers calling Lorna *young lady*), past comedians, karaoke singers, strip shows: strippers named Voom-voom Vicki, Luscious Laurie. The four listened awhile to a gray-haired man sitting on a stool, who pulled hard on a cigarette between the insults he delivered to audience members seated near him, which made the rest of the audience laugh and laugh. Then he sang a song which Lorna would remember for years afterward, a popular tune in England that had become a kind of sentimental anthem. *I just wanna dance the night away . . . with a señorita who can sway.* He didn't so much sing, as croak it. The massive audience filled the big darkened tent with singing, stumbling against one another on their paths to and from the toilets. Their white tank tops glowed lavender under the black lights. Stan and Erleen sang too, gazing again into each other's faces.

Lorna thought: oh where's the harm. This was it, she thought, for these stupefied, sad workers on their holidays. This was it.

Then it was time to go find Sandy Candy. Erleen put her hand on Lorna's shoulder as they walked, her breath ashy and yeasty: Ye'll not believe this, dearie: no one could make it up. Erleen and Stan seemed pulled along by a current, a river of humankind streaming around them. Lorna longed to run away, back to the hotel, but she knew it would embarrass Brad if she insisted on that; it would puncture the symmetry of the four like a flat tire, leave the vehicle of them listing, broken. Some part of her urged her to face her own habitual dread, overcome it, live through it—*it was only a question of living through time, a period of time*—make it a dismissed nothing, relegated to the past.

They paid their cover money—surprisingly steep—and entered an area resembling a circus tent. There was a central, paved floor where spotlights played; young, drunken girlfriends danced the Marguerita with each other. The crowds were packed thick at tiny tables; many more lined the area standing. The whole room seemed to be vibrating. Stan and Brad went off to find drinks, and Erleen and Lorna managed to secure two chairs in the din, at a table near the paved central stage. The music was deafening rock that shrieked and pounded—a raw, jungle pre-saging of something writhing.

A secret ceremony.

It was impossible to be heard unless you screamed.

The men came back and placed drinks before the women. Lorna sat taut. She found she did not want to look at Brad, though he'd been sweetly attentive, stroking her hair, asking several times if she were all right. They waited. The young girls danced in the spotlights. *Hey, Marguerita.* The lights played all around the room and it was clear there was a tremendous wait-ing in the air, smoke hanging cloud-dense, smells of whiskey and beer like moldy bread and stomach acid.

They waited. At midnight a man's English voice on a loud-speaker cheerfully asked all people below the age of eighteen to leave. A great deal of movement and shouting and drunken noise followed as the younger ones, mostly girls, issued slowly from the building, carrying babies and dragging children.

More waiting.

The music pounded, relentless, insistent, jungle drums amplified so that it seemed to shake Lorna by the bones and take over her heartbeat. She felt hot, near to fainting; all the air in the room seemed to have been sucked away by the bodies pressing in. She was aware of Brad's presence somewhere near but did not want to look at him, did not want to see his face. She did not want to see anyone's face or be there but she was there and the faces were all around her. She tried to look at the faces of the strangers. They were drunk, their features blurrily arranged. She wanted desperately to flee, but told herself sharply she had to face off with it, make the long-delayed crossing into becoming the kind of grownup who could allude to events like these with a laugh and turn easily, with all the others, to something else. She had seen a few porn films and magazines: the images always resembled raw pink pork and chicken parts, bound in clear shrink-wrap in supermarket bins. Something in them roused her but mostly made her sad, for she knew a little about the work—that it paid extremely well to women who'd otherwise be on welfare. She knew these women had children and lawsuits and ill-tempered husbands or boyfriends or pimps, that often they shot heroin or speed, that while splayed or hunched and making scripted noises they were most concerned for whether their stomachs were pulled flat, whether their press-on nails would hold, how much money was still needed to buy the next desire, including the drugs.

She'd lived in the world, she told herself.

After what seemed hours a big man came with deep strides through the crowd from a back hallway, and behind the man came a small woman. She wore a long cloak and carried what looked like a portable podium, with little curtained shelves behind it. This she placed before her once the big man (glowering in meaningful sweeps around the room) had cleared a space for her at the center of the crowd. Lorna and Brad and Erleen and Stan were grouped slightly to the right of the petite woman, who stepped quickly, gracefully into the center of the crowd and threw off her cape and stood naked before them all.

The loudspeaker voice screamed: *Live. Tonight. In Doriben, Spain—the world-famous—Sandy Candy*. The crowd boiled with yelling and stomping, shouting and pressing forward.

She was lovely. Her blonde hair was pulled tightly back into a chignon like a ballerina's, her face artfully made up. Lorna thought suddenly of a beautiful Mexican hostess on television commercials in Lorna's own childhood: Aquanetta, a name

Lorna had thought liquid. Aquanetta had been the color of heavily creamed coffee, dressed in brilliant *folklorico* costumes; worn her hair the way Sandy Candy did. She'd exhibited the same exotic graciousness, the same elegant bearing. Sandy Candy could have been a diplomat's wife, giving a ball for the national ballet company of Paris.

In the smooth movement of tossing away her cape—caught mid-air by the big man, who roved his eyes around the crowd with keenness—Sandy Candy flung off a scanty bra, releasing two perfect breasts shaped like full teardrops, creamy and buoyant as a twenty-year-old's. She was now completely nude, a single smooth form before the roaring mass. Lorna felt her heart wring violently. Sandy Candy's body was exquisite, flawless and white, a marble sculpture. Her buttocks were silken, fruity. Her pubis was shorn save for one thin vertical line of close-trimmed blondish-brown hair, which in its own way seemed modest and tasteful as a scarf. The rock music pounded so that no sound besides a continual, throbbing roar could be distinguished, though Lorna was sometimes aware of shouts from the men of *Yeah* and *All Right*, blended into the frenzied pounding. Lorna tried to watch some of the women. They seemed drunkenly pleased yet confused, wobbly; some were staggering. One or two had been dragged out by friends in the act of being sick. A riddle of nature like platypuses: how willfully, blindly, obliteratingly drunk the Brits worked to become.

Sandy Candy walked around the cleared circle, regal, her arms open and lifted like a trapeze artist's—in welcome and acclaim, in proud delight. This was (Lorna saw, dazed) the clear message: pride of skill, pride of beauty. If her witnesses were drunken leerers, if slobbering horniness beat behind the hundred pairs of eyes upon her, if men were going to fall upon their women like dogs when they returned to their beds with the image of Sandy Candy rippling in their skulls, Sandy Candy seemed not to know it. She seemed to be addressing something not present in the stinking, dust-filled arena.

Sixty-three-years-old, Erleen was shouting in Lorna's ear. Lorna could smell the yeasty beer and bourbon on Erleen's breath. *A grown daughter,* Erleen's furrowed mouth bussed her ear like a drunken lover's. Lorna nodded without looking at Erleen, wanting to swat off that wrinkled mouth, swipe at it with a free arm as you might a heavy insect. She had no idea whether Erleen's claims could be true. Either way, what did it prove? Only that Sandy Candy took excruciating care of herself; perhaps she'd had makeover surgery. The woman was beautiful as a china vase.

Sandy Candy stepped back to the center of her clearing, smiled, and suddenly made a folding movement at her middle, bending her knees, raising her pelvis slightly up-and-forward, a pose you might hold to insert a tampon, while her arm reached between her legs. There her hand retrieved an egg, whole and apparently fresh. It looked dry as bone, Lorna could not help noticing. Sandy Candy held the egg aloft, twirling it for all to see, smiling (*this woman is naked,* Lorna thought again)—then paced swiftly to her portable podium to place the egg on one of the curtained shelves behind it. Lightly she stepped again into the center of the clearing, and over the next twenty minutes, with a series of the same quick pelvis-tilts—a posture which stabbed Lorna, because it reduced the delicate ballerina to a peasant in a toilet stall—produced another egg, a feather boa, a length of multicolored silk, a string of flashing colored lights, a British flag, a toy plush rabbit, and eventually a full, capped bottle of Coca-Cola, which Sandy Candy brought to an abashed young man (she trotted eagerly, feather-light, toes turned out, a *corps de ballet* princess) clasping a silver bottle opener, which must also have been removed from herself, and in ladylike miming motions requested he open the bottle for her. She looked like a small naked white doll standing before the weaving, disheveled man, a Tinkerbell. He cracked open the bottle, and she took it from him and poured a bit of soda onto the ground as evidence of the cola bottle's realness, holding her other arm aloft in an arc of weightless grace. While Sandy Candy turned in triumph to the crowd, her back to him, the young man made a show of smelling his hand. The music pounded on, a hellish anvil chorus, and the crowd surged with raucous shouts, screaming and clapping. Sandy Candy danced each new article back to the shelves behind her podium, while the big bodyguard's eyes roamed the assembly like a distempered lighthouse beam.

Lorna had wrapped her arms around herself. She talked to herself in measured phrases. *A long-honed skill.* Stretching and filling the pelvic cavity. Removal by pressure on the lower belly. Use of breath. Placement of objects, powdered for smoothness. Hours inserting the materials so they would emerge just so—so they would not injure. Hours of preparatory time, then walking to the ring of screeching humans with a womb packed so tightly that a false move might have ripped her open inside. There was no question but she believed herself an artist. *What was her name? Alessandra?*

Phrases. *A recreation by humans.* Long-practiced. The world. Other, similar recreations. No one harmed. No theft of civil liberties. Everyone goes away, sleeps it off. Makes a funny story back home. Souvenir, Christmas ornament. No different from junkshop novelties, machines that farted when you put in pennies, plastic penises, oversized ink pens shaped like fully clad women whose clothes disappeared when you turned them upside down. Nothing more. Nothing more.

But Lorna felt as though someone had slapped her, her cheeks stinging as the four walked out the door. The pounding music faded slowly, like a towering monster in deflation. Lorna did not look at Brad or the others, but into the swirling screams of the drunken crowds pushing across the midway. People lurched in and out of shows, burger stands, chip shops. They stepped around vomit on the sidewalks and gutters.

The four said goodnight after Erleen, brushed accidentally by Lorna, spilled French fries and catsup on herself in the elevator. She gave Lorna a hate-filled look.

Lorna and Brad were silent as they walked the few paces to their room. They fit the key into the lock and entered; the weighted door fell shut behind them with echoing finality.

Brad glanced at the clock. It's late, he said.

Yes. Lorna tried to make her voice answer in a matching tone: offhand calm. *Just get into the bed. Get somehow to sleep. It might all be erased by morning. Not his fault, nothing to do with him, not his fault.*

He turned to her when the lights were out.

What is it, he said quietly.

Lorna curled fetus-like against him and sobbed, swallowing her repulsion at the touch of him, familiar as he was.

It's a horror, a nightmare, she wept.

I found it boring, he said. I wanted to leave.

Lorna did not completely believe this, and it pressed a thorn into her head with what it implied—that the act could have interested him, done some other way. But she had no heart to challenge it, and even if she could—even if she could debate him like fucking Alexander Hamilton, what would that accomplish. *Let me fucking out of here.*

It makes me not want to be in the world, she sobbed. The world, including the treacherous body of her husband, seemed to collapse and fold over her in that bed like giant bat wings, black and tented and reptilian, rubbery and sticky. Outside through the heavy curtains, the roars of the drunken revved. Shouting. Firecrackers. A car alarm went off, undulant siren squalls. Someone was rolling a metal beer keg down the sidewalk.

Somewhere in town in a dressing room, Sandy Candy was having a cigarette and a glass of papaya juice, counting her money.

I understand, he said. We'll never do it again.

You don't. You *don't* understand, Lorna cried. We were all part of it. The worst of it. We're responsible. It's like that story, she cried.

What story? Brad took a silent breath, girding for the ordeal: talking her down, talking her through. He was tired, bored, bitterly regretting his mistake. He should have known better. Lorna couldn't watch movies with the least tension in them. She got tearful at television commercials, sorry for trees when a branch was sawed off, sorry for spiders swept into the broom. Harping at him how things might go black on them at any moment, which he could only try to chide her out of. What percentage was there, thinking that way? Yes, right, so she'd lost her mother young; poor kid had to find the body in its bed, cool and blue, mouth sagging at the corners, and yes, the father'd been a tomcat, screwing his way through boredom—a common enough tactic, if not very well thought out. So the mother'd swallowed pills—never considered fighting back or getting help. Brad still shook his head at this. But after a while Lorna's slashed childhood had to sink—*had to*—into the vast lake of everyone's losses. His own dad snuffed too young in a matter of weeks, stomach cancer. You lived a while, you took hits. And truth was that after a certain age, nobody gave a shit. It wasn't compelling. It wasn't some urgent, correctible transgression that had to be *redressed*. Brad wanted a cheerful pal. Lorna was a tender woman who laughed easily, but whose natural mood slipped, without his buoying her, into a kind of baffled sadness. He'd teased her all their years, but sometimes these flayed nerves of hers became a thoroughgoing pain in the ass.

Arrangements had to be made, care to be taken.

That story where the men go fishing, Lorna sobbed. And they see a beautiful naked dead woman, drowned under the cold water in the river where they're fishing. But they've come all that way and taken so much trouble to get there they decide to ignore the dead woman, to report her to the police after they go back, after their fishing is done. Do you remember? They just camp there, fish upstream of her. And then one of the men tells his wife when he gets home, and she cries and cries and runs away from him.

Brad remembered the story, sort of. Lorna read too much. He thought it fed her morbidity. Not to mention the tedium. When he came home evenings tired, his brain felt like a piece of wood. The last thing he wanted was a book review. He was silent.

Then he thought of something, and in hopefulness asked it tenderly as he could.

Is this hormonal?

Lorna shook with sobs. The top of her head pressed his chest. We're the perpetrators, she said, looking up, her face pouchy and slick. We're monsters. A mistake by God. *Big* mistake. She spat these words, rising suddenly. Hiccoughing, she went to gather toilet tissue to stanch her streaming nose. Why wasn't he lacerated, too? Why didn't owning a penis make him sick to his guts tonight? Why didn't it just smack him over the head with its dumb eyeless mystery, leave his teeth chattering?

Why do you love me, she said after she'd lain down beside him again, and they'd been quiet for some minutes.

Because you're the most interesting person I know, he said. I'd be lost without you. You know that.

He did love her, when she wasn't in one of her states like this. He enjoyed her. She had ways of describing things that amazed him. They had fine sex—when she wasn't in one of her states like this. These breakdowns happened rarely, but to live with her was to feel their potential under the surface. Like one of those people who could bleed to death from a minor cut.

Brad could feel himself arriving to that zone in a man's life where what is wanted gets simpler, but also desperately important. Not to hurt anywhere when you got up. Enough sleep, pleasant sex, decent cup of coffee, decent dinner. No complexity, no obstructions as you reached for these things.

Things ticking over.

It was also the zone in which a man understood he had worked hard a long time, and could expect plenty more: a long time of working hard. This gave any pleasures obtained en route a trickier burden. They had to count. Lorna used to tease him about it: *Frolic, damn it.*

But I'm crazy, Lorna was saying. I can't bear what most everyone else seems so well able to bear. Why? Why doesn't that freak you out? She began to cry again.

You always have good stuff to say, he reminded her. I like talking to you.

She absorbed this. She didn't entirely believe it, but she knew he wanted her to. And that he wanted her to, counted for something. Except at bottom she also knew he was too tired to make a change, to sever a pulsing network of family and history so interpenetrated it had become a hybrid creature. They were both too old, too tired to start again. Interviewing, auditioning—it exhausted them both to consider, she knew, even in fantasy. But Lorna knew something else: that if she died, Brad would make sure—furiously, ferociously sure—he did not land someone like her again. He would probably find someone younger, and—undented. Not a single, second thought in her pretty head.

And you don't mind that I'm crazy this way?

I don't mind. I love you.

He felt like a captain at the wheel of a huge liner, inching through razored narrows. Lorna sighed, hiccoughing a little, beside him in the dark. Outside, the howls and jeering grew fainter. In the morning she would force herself to open her legs for him, though right now the thought of it made her ill. And he would remind himself never, never, never to take his wife to a skin show again; that impulse would have to play itself out in some separate room. Meantime they would go find their coffee, read the paper, have a nap. Take a bus to a train and thence to an airplane, and fly away to manageable, above-ground lives. And the days to come, in both their minds, if they resolved it—and here was another impetus for that, perhaps what ultimately made the distress useful, even necessary—if they worked at it, the days would begin clean and glowing again, new and pure as a velvet-soft baby chick.

SAVOIR FAIRE, SAVOIR VIVRE

Nikki had paused at the booth selling maps of the constellations, when the man who would become her first husband saw her.

Indian Summer in the straw-gold hills above San Rafael was dry and warm, filled with scents of trampled grass. In its midst the Renaissance Faire set a jostling peasant world of crafts and music, wet dust, roasting meats and yeasty ales, *papier maché* giants striding along on stilts. Nikki had been strolling the midway in a long cotton sundress made of colorful patches of madras fabric; it tied behind her neck, baring her back, and elasticized around her waist, revealing her creamy arms and bosom to careless advantage. Her cheeks blazed with the heat;

her hair's dark streaks of gold caught the sunlight; eyes followed her as she passed as if she were a riddle that begged solving.

When Brendan saw her she was leaning on the display counter examining the dark blue charts, marveling at the tangled grids of stars: chin in hand, soft cleavage framed in its colorful patchwork casing, her beauty such that the doings around her had slowed. The mapseller stood dazed as if he'd seen real tears trickling down the cheeks of a religious statue.

Brendan O'Callaghan (the native Gaelic for the name meant "strife," and also "bright-headed") was a young lawyer, normally a crisply sensible man. He knew at once, however, that he had never seen anything like Nikki van Klees in his life, and that he never would again. He walked straight up to her and said: I have never seen anyone like you, and I never will again. Brendan was serious and wholesome, with a military haircut. He looked like a yearbook photo of the student voted most likely to succeed. He was to start work the following week as the youngest district attorney appointed in the history of San Francisco. He said to Nikki: Please have something to drink with me.

She stared in fascination at the perfectly sober face. It was so steady, so clear, so bravely serious.

Nikki left the flowerchild streets to marry him. She had run away from home, after high school in Sacramento, to San Francisco, where she took a job as cover artist for *The Guru*, the weekly hippie tabloid. Her folks had disowned her. It was a long shot, going from pauperess to princess, and at first it seemed to work. With Brendan she produced three pretty children, one after the other, and she entered society. Brendan worked like a fiend; never brought the unpleasant details of criminal justice home. They had a chic house in Diamond Heights, private schools for the children, a cook and nanny and maid, vacations everywhere. All Nikki had to do was monitor her babies and look heavenly. The city murmured with admiration for the astonishing beauty of D. A. O'Callaghan's wife.

Nikki told herself it was good. She told her younger sister Hannah, in their furtive phone calls, it was good.

After a while, it wasn't good.

Hannah van Klees sits across from me now in a brasserie, in Paris, France. I am staying here with my fiancé while he teaches a semester-abroad class, and I am still staring at my high school friend in disbelief. I met Hannah this icy March morning utterly by chance, walking in the Jardin du Luxembourg. She is just as I remember her at fourteen, but taller: a large, imposing being in navy cloak and black tights, all hefty shoulders and dense legs. With the cloak she resembles a shockingly athletic nurse. Her straight, sandy hair is still too short, blunt-edged, covered on one side by a navy wool beret; her face's broad bones and pour of freckles, the same. Tiny lines underscore her light blue eyes. She is here to visit her older sister Nikki, who has come to Paris, Hannah says, to paint. I have bundled us into the nearest brasserie (on the Rue de Medicis) and am buying Hannah everything I can think of, to keep her talking. There aren't many English-speaking friends for me here, let alone one I knew as a teenager.

We've started with cocoa and tea, and soon it will be lunchtime.

Hannah looks out the window. She is a professional swimmer: teaches at master's level in a Sacramento health club; she's also a sales rep for a printing supplies company, to support her travel to competitions. She sips her cocoa, wrapping her big white freckled hands around the cup to warm them. She must be sick of people asking what has become of her notorious sister; must keep a dozen versions of the story at the ready, depending how much time there is, and who wants to know. The brasserie noise and espresso steam this busy, freezing day, taut French citizens zipping around with bleak, blank faces, make bulky Hannah even more an apparition before me. Her smile is slow and peevish. I always imagined she'd selected this mannerism in childhood, like a saber or board game token, because what else could you do, having Nikki for a sister.

I gaze at her heavy spray of rust-colored freckles.

Did you ever marry, Hannah? Have kids?

The warmth and coffee smells and cigarette smoke, the steady clatter of dishes, the urgent, shirring voices of other *clients*, enwrap us cozily. Outside it has begun to "spit," fat, random pellets of cold rain which dribble down the window. I have signaled the waiter from afar.

Naw, never married, Hannah says, coloring to the top of her forehead, an effect both charming and alarming. She looks quickly at her cup, then out the window. Too busy. Training, teaching, the sales work and travel.

She looks up. You?

I explain my current, late-blooming circumstance. No kids. One fiancé. Trying to write, and to read all I can. Flaubert in the original. Lots of dictionarying. I am forty. So is Hannah.

And what about Nikki, I finally ask.

Hannah sighs.

Veronica van Klees was the most dazzling girl in school. The one in everyone's pasts. The one everyone was afraid to speak to. You could never come to terms with beauty like that, but even at fourteen you could see that the world was ruled by it. Even now it seems odd that Nikki had issued like most of the rest of us, from people you'd not look twice at, slogging out their lives in a frowsy suburb.

But that was the thing about beauty. That was the way beauty worked.

Veronica. The high school halls are where I first remember seeing her. Sacramento winters brought cold fog and rain; light along the walkways was pearly gray. In that light we glimpsed her: pressing through the milling noise of bodies, forearms holding her books close. The face was what struck you first. To this day I have wondered how anyone deserved such skin. Fresh cream, with a flush of dark rose at the high, broad cheekbones. Vermeer skin. Her features bore the sturdiness and milky light we associate (in paintings, at least) with that part of the world: glowing cheeses, cold brown bottles, still-lifes with lemons and pomegranates. If you half-shut your eyes you could imagine Nikki posed in crisp, winged headdress and collar, standing beneath a window. But all the starched linen in the world could not have concealed the raw petal of her skin, or the blue smoke of her eyes. Her eyes welled, as if seeking relief from a puzzling wound received in another dimension—for which, somehow, the observer felt responsible.

Nikki's face seemed to be listening to private voices, telling her where she could find the destiny she had mislaid—a mission quite beyond those mealy faces milling around her like fish. She walked, it always seemed to me, through a gray wash of nonbeings, as if toward the reverberant heart of her goal: some warm beating place just offstage, where she was meant to be.

In high school days, I felt regret for Hannah. Not pity, but regret. Hannah's features, while clearly sibling to Nikki's, were not beautiful—something Hannah knew very well. We *all* knew it, though of course it was never mentioned. Hannah's hair, chopped in a too-short pageboy, emphasized a too-broad jaw. She was drenched in freckles, as if someone had sloshed a bucket of rust-colored paint at her. Hannah was not ugly, but next to Nikki people could only view her as a kind of goofy pet. Partly it had to do with age, of course. At fourteen in those days, self-image was mossy, like unbrushed teeth. Older kids seemed to own their lives in a breezy, purposeful way. We hoped, chaotically, to pick up clues by gawking. But we were still kids. We played Monopoly and Parcheesi, fixed baloney sandwiches with mayonnaise, stirred Nestle's Quik into our milk. We watched cartoons and monster movies, bought candy bars and comic books. Nikki, on the other hand, was always simply out, or preparing to go out. Going out was her entire life, as far as we could see. I might notice a slice of her sometimes, disappearing behind a door. She left a luscious perfume wake, like gardenias. A scent you wanted to breathe in and in and in.

Gardenias or not, each sister treated the other like a fungus while I was there. For Nikki, I suppose, Hannah was a strewn object she tripped over. And I think Hannah was resigned to this, seeing there was no choice: things were not going to change. That's the part I regretted, for Hannah's sake. But in response she had managed to perfect, even at fourteen, a kind of stoic contempt. Hannah's face, in those days, claimed complete indifference to the fortunes of the fragrant goddess in the next room.

Hannah told me stories when we were kids, about how Nikki was always in trouble with their parents, for sneaking out to see boys. No surprise there. Pity the poor parents. Pity the boys. It was all skewed, skewed from the first in that deepdown way everybody knows—kids know it the way they know fear, or cold—that no one talks about, and no adult admits. Adults can prattle on about fair play, their shreds of righteousness like bedclothes held defensively to the chin. Beauty swipes it all aside, laughing crazily. Beauty torches the place.

I remember walking to Hannah's by myself after school to surprise her, one drizzling October afternoon. (The van Kleeses lived near the high school, and kids still walked everywhere.) The house, of dirty-white clapboard, sat at the end of a street that right-angled into a cul de sac. As I came around that curve into view of the van Klees place I saw something that made me stop and draw back behind where the curve began, to get out of sight as best I could.

Nikki was on the front porch, facing my direction. A young man stood before her, his back to me. Nikki was clasping her suitor's forearms, as if the two were about to dance a reel. She wore a soft sweater-skirt ensemble of light gray, lighter than the clouds that day. Her hair bobbed shinily and her enormous blue-gray eyes, edged in charcoal shadow, gazed up into the face of the young man, whose back was to me. I never saw his face, though I was pretty sure he had to be handsome. It was clear he was trying to kiss Nikki, and she, laughing and joking, was resisting. He would swoop down to press his mouth to her lips or her neck, and she'd curl sideways or lean brightly back, holding him just away and yet at hand, eyes on his. Every so often I heard her laugh, cool and throaty. The young man's movements were quick, and Nikki's resistance, alert. For long minutes I watched this smiling struggle, bits of her laughter drifting out like snatches of music in the chilled, rainy afternoon. I saw, without having words for it then, that the young man was hapless as a baby rabbit in a sack. Something large and queer and ancient was being accomplished, entirely in Nikki's power. It made my stomach feel twisty and sick.

I crept away and walked home.

To me, it seemed that the very beautiful owned a secret. An elusive secret, precious and guarded, of *savoir faire, savoir vivre*. Knowing what to do, how to live. And there in that knowledge, I thought, the anointed few dwelt forever: untouchable, divine.

Do you remember Frank Wheeling—Mr. Wheeling? Hannah hunches forward.

Lunch hour: the brasserie in overdrive. Billowing cigarette and cigar smoke; shouting and clanking; smells of garlic, anchovies, meats, butter. The waiters, young men in their twenties and thirties, sallow and thin with bad skin, sail about at dizzying speed; when they speak to you their cigarette breath is direct. I order *kirs*, and a carafe of rouge. The wine cocktails appear quickly, their lovely rosé pink cheering, like old-fashioned punchbowl punch. Hannah and I clink glasses.

Frank Wheeling had been our school's only art teacher. He used to lean against his open classroom door, watching students come and go: arms folded, one leg crossed in front of the other, toe of a shoe propped upright against the concrete walk, gunslinger style. Black cropped hair, composed face. Smiling at the noisy streams of kids around him like someone enjoying antics in a barnyard—but never cruel. A little tired, maybe. Mr. Wheeling seemed to have dropped from a world far from that of the school. Not constantly fretting about rules and moral imperatives the way other teachers did. His moral center was anchored elsewhere; you could feel that—somewhere we'd not yet been. Of course we were too young to say it that way. Frank Wheeling was an oil painter. He must have stayed up late at night doing his paintings. We knew Mr. Wheeling had a wife and kids, but they never appeared, and we felt, rather than understood, the exotic reality of a man quietly and unflinchingly dedicated to his art. He brought a tolerant kindness to his students, but teaching didn't drive him. He sort of didn't care, in a genial way. If you had some talent, that interested him.

Nikki, it appeared, had some talent. Oils and watercolors. Portraiture and landscapes. She used numbers of thick little strokes, so that the completed whole seemed to vibrate or glitter, from a distance. Hannah only learned of her sister's painting at the end of Nikki's senior year, when Nikki told her parents that Mr. Wheeling advised she go to a special school in Pennsylvania, to develop her gift. The school offered scholarships; he would recommend her. Thomas Eakins had spent time there. Mr. and Mrs. van Klees, simple working souls, were horrified. Mr. van Klees was convinced Nikki's art teacher was a Communist with sexual designs on his daughter. The only art Mr. van Klees allowed for were the mural-style posters offered in his *Military History* magazine, valiant clashes at Waterloo or Antietam or Little Big Horn. His wife stood a few paces back, hands clasped, echoing her husband's wishes; it could never have occurred to her to do otherwise. Nikki stared at them for a couple of inscrutable beats. Then she told her parents they could both go straight to hell, and packed up and left home that same day.

That was when our folks disowned her, Hannah says. It was one of those *we have no elder daughter* numbers. Hannah stretched her mouth in an attempt to grin. Stupid fools. I mean they weren't evil, our folks, but they were rubes. So it was up to me to keep track of her. Every Thursday night we phoned each other at different pay phones, setting the new place up the week before. Sometimes I sent her money. Slipped it from my dad's wallet; God knows the man was clueless enough. They're both dead now, the folks.

She shrugs. Hope they've forgiven me in heaven.

Her smile is lopsided, sardonic. Amused at the lot of them. The wine is doing its job.

So she marries Brendan, I remind Hannah.

After a while Mrs. O'Callaghan soured of shopping at Joseph Magnin and Weinstock Lubin. She didn't care anymore about the luncheons, the spa or the tennis. The people in circles useful to her husband's career, whose names and photographs surfaced like shiny carp in the society pages of the *Chronicle*, had at first intrigued Nikki. But soon they made her rage with boredom. She missed the spontaneous mischief of her friends on the Berkeley streets. She missed doing *Guru* covers, staying up half the night in the cold, dirty offices, drinking jug wine or stale coffee. (Sometimes she still picked up a copy of the paper on the street; it was obviously in decline.) Brendan was a sweet, determined provider, but he had no play in him, no sass. Her children were lovely, but they did not figure at Nikki's absolute center. What figured there instead, as far as Hannah or anybody else could tell, was a kind of unmetness, chewing steadily at her like so many garden snails. Nikki began making forays alone to the De Young Museum or the Legion of Honor, brought home library books about the nineteenth-century painter Berthe Morisot. Sometimes Brendan came home to find her sitting in the back garden by the three-tiered fountain, her pretty shoulders hiccoughing with sobs. Brendan was flummoxed. He wanted his exquisite wife to be happy. He urged her to do her painting right there in the garden; take classes. Drive out to the Marin headlands. Whatever she wanted. And Nikki did try. But psychically she could not cut free of the heavy tent of her family and its trappings. Even if she drove to a different setting she felt them needing her, clamoring, bearing down, Brendan and the children and the house, waiting, wanting. When she tried to so much as envision a canvas the pack of them would crowd of a sudden into her mind like a carful of clowns, honking and squabbling and tumbling.

Nikki packed a suitcase and took a train to New York, to find Frank Wheeling.

Wheeling was by then becoming a name, living in a converted barn near Woodstock. His kids were grown and gone. His wife was amiable, if tired. Nikki stayed with the Wheelings two months, in a carriage house in tall, emerald grass. Mrs. Wheeling gave her warm milk with a little whiskey. Frank showed her his studio, and insisted she sit for a portrait. He hadn't yet moved into photorealism; his style was semi-abstract in bold strokes—like Picasso's late portraits.

Frank Wheeling was an observant man. Somewhere between high school and her flight from O'Callaghan, Frank guessed, Nikki's impulse to do art had placed itself at odds with her need for adulation. Talent was one thing, but to work it hard was lonely, and it was—well—work. Nikki still indulged a young person's comfortable habit of holding her own potential just beyond reach, where it could flash like a coin through water. This standoff was attractive, Frank knew, so long as one was young. Perhaps because Nikki was in no state to hear it during her convalescence at the Wheeling home, Frank did not spell it out to her then. (He explained to Hannah as best he could, when she contacted him years later.) Frank only told Nikki at the time *you are going to have to make some tough choices and stick by them*, and Nikki thought she understood. The portrait of her that survives from those days (in Hannah's possession now) shows a woman of beauty and grace but disjointed, akimbo.

A divorce was swiftly granted to Attorney O'Callaghan. His friends wondered why Brendan had sought full custody of his children.

They were not told that Nikki had asked Brendan to take them.

Was there another marriage, I ask.

Hannah shifts slightly on her hard chair. Afternoon smudges the windows. The soup is gone, the omelette gone, the wine and *salade,* and we've twisted the remains of the baguette to bits. A young waiter gaunt as a junkie teeters over us. *Du café? dessert?* Absolutely. And for my friend here, if you please, an Armignac. Hannah cocks her head. C'mon, dear, I say. We're celebrating. The liquor that arrives is the color you would obtain if you could melt bars of Fort Knox gold with late autumn leaves, then strain the mixture clear. You half expect to smell leaf smoke when you inhale at the snifter.

Hannah's pale freckly skin wears a moist sheen, and her eyes are watery.

There is a man named Lorne. Lorne Pike, she says, exhaling slowly.

She swirls the Armignac in its glass.

Lorne was a little older than both sisters in grade school. He'd moved to another district by high school, so the girls had lost track of him. Even as a boy he was handsome and hearty; his hair buzz cut on top and slicked back on either side. Even then Lorne's walk had been loose and his chest strong, his grin a warm, shy promise. Once he followed both girls home from school (at eager, polite, confused distance). Young Hannah, whose wiry hair stuck out at stiff angles like Raggedy Ann's, had been terrified, her heart punching from her chest, because she secretly loved him. Nikki, all blonde curls, with the sadistic radar for this sort of thing that is common between siblings, had thrown down her books once inside the house and raced back out to the front porch. *Hannah loves you,* she had brayed to Lorne, who'd stood astounded on the sidewalk. Then Nikki had turned and run back in to confront her little sister with a triumphant smirk.

Hannah's eyes are far away.

Jesus, I say.

Lorne showed up again—much later, she says after a moment, looking deeply into the amber shapes forming and reforming in her Armignac.

How did he find her? I ask.

The lunchtime crowd has thinned, leaving those whose lives' arrangements, fortunate or not, allow them to bide. Most smoke. Some read a book or newspaper. A couple of old women, powdered and expensively dressed, sit side by side, gazing out the window at streetlife and weather. The waiters have faded into the kitchen or ducked out to the cold, where they smoke and banter and harass passing girls.

After the divorce Nikki signed up for classes at the Art Institute in the city, Hannah says.

The Institute offered scholarships, and Mr. Wheeling's letter got her in. Nikki decided not to see her Berkeley friends, because she thought they would distract her from her studies. She rented a flophouse room on California Avenue, and found a job at an old movie theater a few doors down. Her classes were tolerable and she worked at her paintings, but progress felt exasperatingly slow. Her fellow students were geeky, the neighborhood cold and dirty, her movements tightly circumscribed. She had to take a bus or BART train across the bay to visit her children, which happened seldom. (Brendan O'Callaghan had married again quickly, this time quite successfully, to a brisk, attractive young woman who was vice president of a well-known computer corporation in Palo Alto.) Nikki was selling tickets at the moviehouse one day for a reprise of "Fantasia," watching the pearling light of the sky through her ticketbooth windows, the piled angel-hair clouds backlit by sun in a Raphaelite manner—when a dark figure stepped between her eyes and those clouds, in the manly form of Lorne Pike.

How quickly time collapsed when you beheld the grown man who'd resulted from the boy you knew! He was himself, vital and well, and yet life had scribbled all over him, like markings on a cutting board. He was an architect. He was divorced. Taking in a movie, he said, during a break in the AIA conference at Moscone Center.

Taking in. Lorne said these words with shy bravura, as if to prove his worldly nonchalance. What did the two know about each other? Exactly nothing. What had they in common? Zero, on surface.

But Nikki was tired, lonely, and broke. She was also bored. It seemed harmless to walk down to Van Ness for a drink with him. Lorne was amazed by her beauty, the more haunting now that fatigue made faint blue hollows at her Vermeer cheeks and around her smoky eyes. She wore a black cotton sweater and a pair of loose dungarees, no makeup at all, and her hair—always the harbinger of her spirit—hung limp, of no color you could name. Her lips unadorned were a faint lavender, like those of a child taken chill in a cold pool. Nikki smoked a cigarette and watched Lorne across the table in the fern bar where they sat, as he outlined his days. Time had treated him well—or he had known how to treat himself well. Same tan, same easy grin. He looked like a cowboy who owned a yacht. Still a bit of a mouth-breather, she noticed—always sounding as though his nose was plugged, but this had been strangely sexy in a country music kind of way when he was a kid, and still was. Lorne made plenty of money. He'd dated around. He liked to go trout fishing at certain secret spots in the lower Sierras, liked to cook, built tables and shelves for fun, saw his retired parents every so often—but here Lorne stopped. They were drinking strong Manhattans, almost tea-colored, a red maraschino cherry floating inside each tumbler like a diabolical eye. They were already a goodly way into second rounds, a point at which many decisions become wondrously clear.

Lorne looked Nikki in the eye and performed the conversational equivalent of yanking the tablecloth in a single whipcrack.

For Christ's sake, Nikki. Why don't you just marry me and dump all this scratching around. I need someone. You need someone. I've been nuts for you ever since we were kids. I'll pay for everything; take you everywhere. We'll buy a condo here. You can do your painting. Aw, Nikki, look at the way you're living.

You need someone to look out for you, Lorne said softly.

I'm him. I'm the guy.

She looked at him, through smoke.

It might have worked, except that Nikki became pregnant straightaway.

One of those everyday mishaps, common as water from a tap. Lorne had never had children: he longed for a child, begged his new wife to have their baby. He swore he would take on the work. He insisted it was do-able, pledged his life on it. And after the baby came, he'd—why, he'd take them all to Tahiti.

As Hannah talks, I can easily see it. Cool seawind, palms and banyans, dappling light. One of those private, thatched cottages you see in magazine ads. A cord strung between the cottage and a palmtrunk, on which their swim things hang to dry: the baby's tiny, tiny pink T-shirt. I can see Nikki step from the cottage in a white camisole with ruffles along the straps, a loose white skirt to her knees. Feet bare, tan and smooth, toenails painted pearly tangerine. A white plumeria with deep yellow streaks tucked behind one small ear. Gold and silver highlights competing over the surface of her hair, backlit by morning sun: the effect of a halo.

A face that curses itself.

I walk Hannah to her hotel. It's on the Rue Jacob. Not so terribly far, when you have a lot of food and wine and cognac to numb you. The early dark is bearing down, the cold deepens, but by now we are well-heated from within; our mufflers wound around us in a pile, up to the nose. No stars. Day or night, this freezing, gray uni-weather—*grisaille*—clings obstinately for months, making people despair until the first brave yellow daffodils poke up, trembling and dazed, in parks and gardens. We pass the majestic Odeon, lit as if for a production of *Antigone* right there on its steps—then along the Boulevard St. Germain. It is the hour when the city shudders with a great flush of transitions: the world of day to the world of night. Charging vehicles, diesel fumes, crowds of walkers clutching flowers and bread, dogs on leashes, howling children pulled along by the hand.

Hannah paces beside me, looking thoughtful and drained. I know there is a last part yet to hear, the Paris part. Maybe it isn't right, my needing to know so badly; maybe it's a little indecent. But something is flitting through Hannah's words, flicking its ghost-tail at me.

I want to stand it still a minute.

Nikki had the baby, Hannah is saying. A little girl. Named for me.

I look at her, but she is keeping her face toward the sidewalk.

They tried to make it work, Hannah says. Lorne helped her all the ways he promised. He built them a house. But finally Nikki couldn't keep on with it. Spent hours at the front window, nights after Lorne and the baby were sleeping, looking at the lights of town, drinking brandy. Doodling with a finger on the glass, in the steam her breath made. Said she felt like she'd doublecrossed herself again. Rerouted herself again.

Rerouted?

From what she was supposed to really be, Hannah says. Really be doing. Her art, I guess. Her painting.

Hannah says the words like someone who has heard them so often, for so long—perhaps they've been thrown at her in fury—they have accreted like coral, become boulders in the apartment of her mind. She maneuvers around them exhausted, one hand stretched out to touch them lightly as she passes, marking her way.

Did Nikki divorce Lorne, too?

We are walking fast to stay warm. The sky is starting to spit again.

No, Hannah says, in a puff of visible breath. She never bothered. She just asked him to let her run away. Lorne said okay—I mean, what good would it have done him to lock her up, keep her like a prisoner. He takes care of little Hannah. A sweet kid: freckles like mine. They're back in Sacramento now. I spend as much time over there as I can. Drive Little Hannah home from daycare. Bring them stuff.

Nikki gave me some grief about it, she says.

Nikki telephoned Lorne's house from Paris, one recent afternoon.

Hannah answered.

What're *you* doing there, Nikki's voice asked thickly, without preliminaries, through the porous stillness of the connection. Where's Lorne?

I'm visiting, you ninny. What d'you think? Lorne's still at work. I've just brought Little Hannah home from daycare. Wanna say hello? She's watching cartoons.

Pause.

Are you having an affair with my husband?

Nikki, are you crazy? I'm your daughter's auntie. You left your husband, by the way, remember? Little Hannah doesn't know her mother's fucking *face*.

Don't think you can try to replace me, Hannahbanana, Nikki murmured. It was the murmur, its sudden weakness and confusion, that told Hannah Nikki was drinking. Hannah tried to calculate. Early afternoon in Sac meant wee hours in Paris.

Nikki, what's going on? Is somebody with you? What d'you need?

I need to talk to Lorne.

Lorne's at work, Nikki. Is it money?

Silence. Hannah thought she could hear Nikki crying.

Nikki, let me come over. I have to fly to a meet next week. I can arrange a stopover. I'll bring some money. From Lorne and me both.

Don't try to nice me to death, now, Hannah. You can't keep it up, being the Virtue Queen all your fucking life. It's so boring, Hannah.

Hannah? Hear me? It's *boring*.

Nikki was crying.

Little Hannah—she says she wants to be a swimmer.

Hannah's voice is low as we walk in the dark.

Lorne Pike is a *saint*, Hannah says with sudden vehemence.

I am quiet. I see that Hannah still loves him, secretly and hopelessly; this earnest man who must think her the kindest sister in the world.

Lorne sent Nikki here, Hannah adds. To study and paint. She asked him to. Nikki told him, *Paris is very important to me.* So far he's put up with it, but I don't know as he'll put up with it forever. Would you?

She jerks her face toward me when she says it. Maybe she envies anyone who doesn't have to carry her ruined sister's baggage around day and night. I stammer no, I guess I wouldn't likely put up with it. At least not for long.

She's studying with someone from the École des Beaux Arts, Hannah says. One of those students who gives lessons on the side. Probably a kid; probably falling for her. Wheeling still writes her sometimes; says he might come visit.

Hannah sounds like she is counting the pieces still standing on a chessboard.

But Nikki's not—quite the way you remember her, Hannah says carefully, after a pause. I saw her last night; I'll see her again tonight. She's kind of . . . burnt. She's been living hard; says she doesn't care so much anymore. How she looks, I mean.

I try to consider a burnt Nikki. And at last the ghostly thing I have been struggling to make out in Hannah's account, looms forward, and it is simple enough. Something I have always known but never put words to, like a melody heard lifelong without lyrics: that an infantile character, a small and crimping soul, uglies up a woman or man, god or goddess—very soon, very fast, and for all time. Once you figure it out you never see them any other way. And you steer far around them after that as if they were a deep hole, thankful to be at safe distance—sorry for those occasional poor bastards who fall in.

Sorrier still, for her family.

I don't believe Nikki is trying to become un-beautiful. That would rule out too much. Better a passport that opens some doors, than no passport at all. Better to go on to the last, flirting with your own brilliant potential. Nikki is probably just finally showing her age, like other mortals.

But it must be a terrible blow to a goddess.

Hannah, why don't you hate her?

We have arrived to the portico of her hotel, our hair damped down, coats spattered. Cars roar around us, headlights beading light on wet pavement. The endless traffic makes a white noise, like an ocean.

My old friend stops and looks at me, puzzled. Tears mix with rain on her broad freckly cheeks, only now all the freckles have melted away in the weak streetlights and dark cold, so that her face looks like white marble, one of those early-century carvings above the doors along the ornate streets. A pale mask.

How can I hate her? Hannah says. I have to try to help her. She is my sister, says Hannah simply, turning toward the hotel's glass doors. She stops and turns back, takes my hand in both of hers, pats it absently. We're like space-suited astronauts, our gloved hands like paws. Goodbye, she says. Thank you for the meal.

Then she slips from my sight.

I stand blinking under the starless night. An accordian has started up somewhere.

Hannah's sardonic manner is a foil: her sister is a *puera aeterna*, and Hannah will never shirk her. In my mind the goddess Nikki dwindles to a discarded mechanical toy with one repeated, rusty gesture. The fact that Nikki is somewhere in Paris tonight, smoking or staring out a window or at a canvas or at yet another luckless mentor, doesn't matter. I no longer care what she looks like. I will find the nearest métro entrance, to descend, and be carried away.

THE SUN ON THE GANGES

Four people sat at dinner in a suburban home, and conversation turned to the days of the doctor's medical school studies in Bologna.

It was a singularly happy time, the doctor told his friends, because of the civilized mien with which the *professores* conducted their business. Bologna is a jewel of a city, he told them. Wherever you turned, beauty laughed back at you. Beauty draped, beauty radiating, beauty strewn like shattered opals in careless brilliance. The pinkish walls of porticoes in diffuse sunlight, all marbley veneers and ancient cracks, the expanses of warm, flat-stoned piazzas and cool shadowed passageways, stunned the observer, ruining you for any other place.

All their studies and exams were conducted in Italian, continued the doctor, whose name was William. And surprises, he said, ambushed you. It was not uncommon in the middle of an oral exam, as morning edged toward noon, said Will, for the *professore* to suddenly stop his student mid-recitation: "Do you like pasta?"

The student would blink.

"You heard me—*do you like pasta?*" the professor would press his young charge.

Of course the student liked pasta.

"And how do you like it, exactly? With an *al fredo* sauce perhaps, or maybe in a little butter with sliced garlic and shrimp and red peppers, or sausage? A scrape or two of fresh *parmigniano reggiano*? Coarse black pepper? A nice chunk of bread, and the olive oil to dip?" By then the student would be salivating, nodding mutely.

Watching and listening to Will as they sipped wine at the candlelit table were his wife Penney, who was a decorator, Mark, who taught history at the nearby college, and Mark's wife Reese, an office manager for a local computer outlet. Will imitated the professor's intonations with the flatly deadpan punches given Italian inflection of English, by Americans who satirize it.

"Then-eh we go-eh to lonch-eh now, eh? We do the exam-eh to*morrow*."

And with that, Will told them, the grateful student and his amused examiner would repair to a good *buca* for a long, leisurely meal, to include some fresh antipasti, a nice valpolicella, and finally syrup-strength espresso with a couple of serious cigars. They would at last bid one another fare-you-well and stagger off for a deep afternoon's sleep in their respective quarters— by which time of course it would have become evening, and time to think about the coordinates of a lovely dinner.

How you got through med school I'll never understand, snorted Reese, a rather sharp woman accustomed to taking daily charge of a number of odious chores that reproduced themselves constantly, like a rampant mold. She brought her lunch every day and ate it while reading in the car. It was husband Mark who befriended people on ships and trains and air-planes; Mark who loved to entertain. He had convinced himself, and Reese, that he was born into the wrong country and the wrong era; he missed a *polis*, or town hub, where community gathered nightly. So they held regular dinners like this one, little substitute-*polises*, with streams of guests from different portions of their pasts. Penney had been one of Mark's night-class students years ago; night class tended to draw an older, married crowd intent on bettering itself. She was a compact, erect woman with bobbed blond hair and half-moon specs; these she peered over with alert patience. Penney had sat forward in Mark's class, taking pages of notes in her meticulous, childishly round hand. She had admired Mark's erudition, his ability to rattle off with relish the highlights of human doings at any given span along the centuries—she had decided this was a dimension she and her doctor husband were missing from their lives—a furnishment, if you will; something one could pull from its storage nook like a good bottle of spirits. Penney was credulous, kind, and cheerful. In off-hours she leafed through magazines, cooked, or took runs with Sadie, a giant, brown-and-white boxer with a questioning, wounded expression and exceptionally soft fur. Sadie was curled on the kitchen linoleum now, pug face resting on extended front paws; leary eyes fixed on the seated humans. Reese was fond of Sadie—a gentle, coltish creature—but wondered how there could possibly be enough reassurance in the world to quash the wet anxiety brimming in the dog's eyes. Penney lavished love on the animal, fed it choice food, took it places. Will cared for little apart from the dog and his wife and making money. He tended to watch late-night cable porn after Penney went to bed.

The two couples now saw each other perhaps twice a year, alternating weekends at each other's homes—mainly at Mark's and Penney's urging. Will went along with what his wife demanded, though he loathed most people on principle. Reese tried to bear the visits for her husband's sake. Penney and Will were lately furnishing a gigantic new home in the most expensive neighborhood of their city, about one hundred miles to the north. Mark and Reese lived in a town noted on state maps for its natural hot springs, in a worn '30s bungalow in an old, tree-lined neighborhood near the town's high school. Reese barricaded herself in the bedroom with her reading while Mark sat on the front porch, smiling and nodding at passersby.

Penney watched her husband as he spoke. She'd heard Will's stories many times, but never protested his telling them—because they were his, and because the code of wifely attitude stipulated a husband should shine in their friends' regards. Reese could not stop staring at the diamond perched on Penney's wedding ring, the biggest she'd ever seen. It seemed to be exploding volcanically from the gold band, its broad-cut facets framing a turmoil of clear, white and electric-blue light. Reese didn't so much want the diamond as she wanted to dwell inside the diamond. Inside that light. Molten, exploding into itself geometrically.

She finally tore her eyes from the intricate blue-white flashes.

Exactly how *did* you make it through med school, Will? Reese asked.

Same way everybody else did, he smiled around at them all. Partying and cramming. Will's smile was faintly chilly and exaggeratedly, almost loonily simple. Will always addressed listeners, Reese thought, as if they were slightly retarded; as if basics of human life needed to be explained in large, cartoon gestures. The contempt in this manner seemed garish to Reese, but Will apparently believed it well-cloaked—unaware he might be telegraphing anything more than a kind of avuncular daffiness. Reese knew two other adult men with this precise, shaming habit; both were scientists. She assumed Will had acquired it during years of doctoring. Mark seemed never to notice, or if he did, shouldered blankly past it in his eagerness to talk economics and politics. And Penney must no longer have registered such broad notes of her husband's public behavior, thinking only in the practical language she shared with him—of money, and its allocation. The doctor and his wife had long ago learned they could not conceive children, and to Reese it seemed they'd spent the rest of their days vigorously walling off that void, then building a gigantic monument on top of it. New homes, many cars, boats, high-end gadgets. Penney seemed crisply determined to be pleased by these spoils. But in Will, Reese sensed a listlessness—rooted in something so deeply and disconsolately cold it gave her a fleeting spasm of alarm, like a small animal of prey.

Will still did occasional surgery on-call—just this week he had reattached a man's finger—but for the most part stayed with a practice he'd settled into for sheer convenience: diagnosing people who were trying to get medical releases from their jobs. These were types long experienced at the game of it, who managed to win surprisingly often—to make a life of being excused from work, with pay. The injuries they complained of were complex, rarely visible, and difficult to prove, often involving obscurely referred pain, unlikely pathologies of muscle and bone and nerve. Will was out to foil them. Night after night he wrote up his charts. Will's patients were often grossly obese, without much formal education, and frequently arrived to the examining room eating a candy bar or drinking through a straw from a gigantic, Big Gulp Slurpee. They'd keep eating, or slurping, while he examined them.

Will was a bitter Republican.

Of course, he was telling his dinner companions, the Bologna students were insane. Smart, though. They hardly studied, yet swept their exams. Exuberant. Everybody a little mad there. Professors, too. I remember one, Will said, who climbed into the classroom through the window, gave a magnificent lecture, and climbed back out. It was a good school, he smiled again.

Will, tell them about Goldy, Penney said suddenly.

Mark's gaze, glittering candlelight on the lenses of his horn-rims, swam back into focus. Stories were good: Mark liked stories. Anything that spirited him away. Especially to Bologna, where even the train station was glorious. He took a sip of spicy zin from his wineglass, now clouded with greasy imprints. Hell yes, tell us, he said.

Something flitted across Will's face and his eyes cast a brief, dry question at Penney.

Good old Goldy, Will said.

Good old Goldy, Penney nodded.

Reese pushed back from the table and folded her arms in front of her. It was a warm autumn evening. All the windows were open; a cricket pulsed soft, high tones. Occasionally cars passing out front popped the walnuts that had cascaded to the street, sounds like little muffled gunshots. Sadie raised her head quickly at these, metal tag jingling around her dense, muscled neck, pronouncing a low, indignant *rowf*—then resettled, brows troubled, wet eyes panning both directions.

The candles burned steadily, at odd moments hissing with a tiny flick of spark as some micro-anomaly interfered with wax and oxygen. The soft, upright yellow flames threw the group's faces into shadowy *noir* sendups of themselves.

Who, please, was Goldy? Reese inquired, reaching to stack the dirty plates nearest her. She'd start running the hot water and soap in five minutes, she told herself. Wash up while the others gabbled. Then excuse herself.

A fellow student, answered Will. His voice had quieted. He seemed to be gazing at a space of air just above the dirty plates.

And? Briskly, in case this was another of Will's protracted jokes.

Goldy was brilliant, Will said slowly, after a moment. So brilliant he scared the professors. He never seemed to study. He missed class or came to class late, looking like hell. But he always aced his exams. Sometimes I saw him arguing with the *professores* after class, correcting some principle they'd taken for granted. They always looked worried when he walked away, Will said, smiling a little, still looking at the space at solar-plexus level above the table.

Was he nice? Reese asked. Was he obnoxious? Where was he from?

Goldy was wild, Will kept saying, shaking his head. Wild.

The room was dark, the empty night outside deeply black without a moon. No other lights were on in the house; the four seemed to be floating in a smooth bubble exactly large enough to contain them, an egg of space kept aloft by the feathery yellow candle-glow.

Goldy was from Canada, Will said. But he knew Italy. He would take us out drinking sometimes, to these little hamlets far out beyond the town in the countryside, or up these hill-side terraces. And in every single bar we entered—every single one—the bartenders knew Goldy. Hailed him with emotion, like they'd known him all their lives. All the regulars at the bars knew him too, greeted him like a lost brother. Will paused to let his listeners digest this. Not only, Will said, did those bartenders and customers all seem to know Goldy, embrace him and clap him on the back like he was MacArthur or something. Every single bartender took down from the wall above the bar—I swear, in every place we stopped—a private mug that was Goldy's own. His own personal drinking mug. Every bar in these far-to-hell holes in the wall, Will said.

He turned his face, a furtive moment, toward Reese.

Can you see what I'm saying, he said.

Reese looked at him in wonder. Will's remarks had always before been cool and ironic, verging on cruel, and in all the years of visiting with Penney and Will the four had made sure to get drunk as fast as possible, because it helped them briefly overcome their looming differences—the fact that were it not for the decorator and the teacher, the four would be having nothing to do with each other. Alcohol was a precious lubricant, Reese had more than once reflected. Tired as she was—late as it was, as much wine had gone down—she tried to pinch herself awake. It was the first time she'd ever heard Will speak like someone who honestly wanted to tell you something.

What'd he look like? Reese asked.

Different ways at different stages, Will answered. When we were just starting out, he was a good-looking guy. Younger than the rest of us. Wild brown hair; sometimes it flew around like Leopold Stokowski's; sometimes tamer, like Bobby Kennedy's. Never could get the part in his hair straight; that always drove me crazy. Clothes too big for him. Skinny kid, but his face was smooth. Big nose. Young boy's mouth. Eyes that looked at you, really looked. But there was—well, this weariness to him. Didn't fit his years. Like he was struggling—

Will took a breath, visibly mortified. He exhaled the rest of the sentence.

—struggling with some kind of comprehension that, uh, gave him pain. Not a physical pain, of course, Will added quickly, coloring.

He stared glumly into the remains of his dessert, a fluffy tiramisu Penney had picked up at a designer bakery. Now it looked like a melted party dress.

Reese marveled. When she and Mark stayed with them, Will sat reading a newspaper while Penney prepared the meal. None of the host's gestures. Not a *can I get you anything, what would you like with your eggs, how about those Seahawks.* Nothing. A flat, silent line. Reese remembered wandering during one visit amid the couple's bookshelves until she'd found a tiny, framed photo of Will's late father, also a doctor. The old-fashioned frame, gilt with scalloped edges, was speckled with dark rust. Will's father stood full length in the photo against a manicured boat in a harbor, arms at his sides. The father's face was that of a warrior-chief facing into the north wind: chiseled, dry, implacable as a tomb. All the external noise of the world fell away from a gaze like that, which so clearly eliminated any use for all the external noise of the world.

Reese imagined a little boy trying to please such a father.

But Goldy wasn't always brooding, Will continued. Sometimes he would sing to us on the way to dinner. A bunch of us would be walking along the *trattoria* around dusk. Maybe it was about looking forward to eating, or the guys being together, or the pale light on the city as evening came, that rose color everywhere, pigeons lifting and falling—some inspiration would hit him now and again. And he would just stop right there and open his mouth like it was a big horn, and *boom.* Goldy knew opera, all the arias—he could sing you anything. Had a gorgeous voice. Tenor.

Mark cocked his head slightly, ruddy and mild. Enough wine always turned flamboyant Mark into a softened presence, a musing Buddha.

What would he sing? Mark asked.

Scarlatti, once, said Will. *Gia' Il Sole Dal Gange*, which is a hard piece to pull off. Full of tricky breathing and trills. Great phrasing. You'd only believe it if you'd seen it—this skinny young kid booming it out in the middle of the street—

What do the words mean? Reese asked.

Will's eyes angled up to a thinking corner, like a schoolboy's.

O'er the Ganges now launches / the sun-god his splendour. How brightly, how brightly it shineth. Those are the first lines, anyway. We would stop and stand around him. Sometimes we'd lift him up and carry him along on our shoulders for a ways, everybody laughing and yelling *bellissimo*.

Reese could see it. A great bronze shield, rough-hewn, a perfect sphere at its center, rising in whiteness, turning to bronze as it rose, throwing bars of light from its hammered facets in all directions, across water and land. A mighty gong.

I remember a Bononcini, too, Will was saying. *Per La Gloria D'Adoravi*—this rich, flowing theme. Goldy would just stand there and close his eyes, that crazy hair of his sliding around as he opened his arms and delivered the songs, sweating into his shirt. I'm telling you, those notes were sustained. And pure, Will said, looking at but not seeing his listeners. From such a skinny kid. Wonderfully pure.

Reese couldn't believe what she was hearing. This, from the man who reviled welfare recipients as primary agents of evil. She sighed with a raising and sinking of shoulders. Difficult, but there it was. Someone had once reminded her that Nazis had listened to Mozart in between execution sessions.

Goldy trained early in music, in Toronto, Will said. Decided on medicine later. Matthias was his real name. Family name was Goldberg; both parents musical. Mother started him on piano before he could speak. I heard his dad died right about then, when Goldy was little, and Goldy developed the idea that he'd make it up to his mom for that, for the loss of the father—by doing medicine, fixing up others, Will said. Also, Goldy wanted to make her some money. Kept a photo of his mother in his room, I remember. And one of himself, too, as a little smiling baby. I couldn't figure out why he kept that one of himself. I asked him about it, the baby photo, when I was visiting his room. Why d'you keep that around? I asked him.

I have to see the spirit as it began, he told me. *In its nakedness. Be reminded*, he said. Will shrugged. That was how Goldy said it. He was making tea in his dorm room at the time, I remember. Room was tiny. Books stacked up all around. The few clothes he wore—over and over, heavy wool stuff, even if weather was hot and humid—hung on pegs in the wall. A particular smell to Goldy's clothes—not unpleasant. (Will said this with slow surprise, as if the information were only just striking him.) Sort of like pastry. Had a little camp stove in there to heat his water; dozens of bags of dried leaves. Always offering me these foul teas he'd brew. Special herbs. Dark as vinegar. Smelled like crap, those teas did. Healthgiving, he told me.

Will made a *search-me* face.

I stared at his baby photo awhile. Looked like a typical baby photo to me; grinning little pudgy guy propped on a blanket on his belly, elbows holding up his chest and head, looking up at the camera laughing. Eyes all crinkled up.

Reese had a hand supporting her chin, forefinger over her lips.

Good old Goldy, Penney said again, shaking her head. Reese caught a tone in it.

What happened after the beginning? she asked.

Will, who was a gangly man, seemed unable to find a comfortable position in his chair. He glanced as if for help toward the windows, which offered only opaque black around a faint reflection of candleglow.

Goldy got involved with an African death mask, he said.

Reese sat up. He *what*?

That's right. What I said. Will stared at the tablecloth.

Will was behaving, Reese decided, like a man who was being pinched very hard under the table by an invisible hand.

Found it at a flea market, Will said. Wandering around the city in one of his trances, I guess. Bizarre-looking thing; black, dusty. God knew what-all it was made of. Must've been old. Eyes seemed to look nowhere and right at you at the same time. Goldy talked a long time with the guy he bought it off, a blue-black man, Goldy told me, in some ratty stall set up by a chunk of medieval wall. Seems the guy persuaded Goldy the mask had powers. Goldy hauled it back to his room and hung it opposite his bed. That was the beginning of the end, Will shook his head.

What do you mean? What happened? Reese felt like not enough air was being allowed into her lungs. Her mind ricocheted with fragments of ochre light and crumbling stone. Will seemed to be longing to wriggle his way out of the account as if it were a tight, itching shirt. Which of course it was for Will, who dismissed the slightest emotional component in anyone's conversation with a look that was a surgical knife-slice.

I'm saying, Will said heavily, that Goldy got involved with the mask.

Could you *please* explain to me what *got involved* means. Reese wanted to shake him. Her face had warmed, and the room felt squishy and steamy.

Goldy got weird on us. He spent hours in his room, staring at the mask. Meditating? I don't know. Just—Will nearly held up an arm to deflect Reese's face—staring at it. Hours and hours. He started to look paler and thinner, and Goldy'd never eaten a lot to begin with. He stopped going out with us. Never talked or sang anymore. Stayed away from classes. When I did manage to get him out for a drink, he'd go on to me about the mask.

All Will's words now seemed to Reese to be swirling together and funneling fast down an inevitable, sucking hole.

What finally happened, she said.

Ah, he shot himself, Will said, waving a hand in the air.

The four sat with this.

Family? Reese wondered.

Will shook his head.

Mother was dead by then. A cousin, an older woman, came over to fly the body back to Canada. I talked with her a little while she was there. Told me she'd been expecting it. Goldy had been phoning her collect for years, she said, all hours, from different phone booths. Jabbering away. Had an idea his own death was near. Some complicated formula he'd worked it out by.

Silence.

Will sat emptied, his wretched dispatch finally pried loose.

Goldy went into the diamond, Reese thought slowly.

Entered that hypnotic space. The molten white center. Probably *lived* there toward the last. Or maybe the white center entered him, blinding him, suffusing him. Too much voltage for his circuits. No surge protector. Reese felt queasy. She could suddenly envision a stream of humans ribboning back into the past like a patient, infinite waiting line—and no one knew what they were waiting for. No one toward the front of the line would ever quite know what had really happened way back at the rear. Except by rumor, by false or faulty stories, and eventually those, too, would disappear. Goldy was dust, mashed to drifting motes, fading already in the minds of even those whose memories still had any hold of him.

Brandy? Mark cleared his throat. Anyone?

Not for me, thanks, Penney said. Reached my quota. She rose cheerfully. 'Night, everybody. Terrific dinner. She glanced down at Sadie, hands on hips. How's about a quick walk, Missy? Sadie scrambled up at once, white chest erect, ears straight, stub-tail ticking. Her metal tag jingled as she followed Penney out.

Mark was already lifting the cognac from the cupboard.

Reese wanted to yell at them. *You can't just write him off like that. You should have begged him to explain his putrid old mask.* You should have drunk his disgusting tea. You should have begged him to stay on, goddamn it. Why, why did there always have to be this—this *pall* that the few angels we ever get, have to fall into, she wanted to yell, while the rest of us just stand around and watch?

In next instants Reese knew very well that she herself could never have endured tending to any Goldy. Never've begged him to stay on. It would have emptied her. The *savants* were the hardest, Reese knew from student days and former lovers: only the young could tolerate them a while. Soon even the young became old with it— the inexhaustible neediness, the futility. Your nerves taut and raw, waiting for the next awful instant when the *savant's* low flame flared into a firewall. All of it wore you to a daze and finally to bitterness, and even the young would at last have to turn away.

Mark was pouring amber liquor into little glass snifters. Will, he said, I happen to have here two exceptional cigars. Ready?

Excellent, said Will, eager with relief. I'm there. He stood, stretching.

Still Reese wanted to rave at them. Can't you remember we're all dust ourselves here in about five minutes? Out there with the leaves. Back into potting soil. We have no time. We have no *time*, she wanted to wail.

Reese said nothing. Years of accrued history in her body told her body to go to bed. Outside the cricket still sang, each note pulsing like a tiny wink of light.

Good night, fellows, she called.

But the men were already gone.

She washed the dishes, brushed her teeth and entered the bedroom, which smelled of cool sheets, hair and skin, night air. She pressed the door behind her, groping in the dark to her side of the bed. Reese sat and let out a breath, the ink-blue night striping the window's slanted blinds before her. Like a plane crash, like a meteor shower, the Goldys of the world came and went. Nights would continue to visit in stately succession, like shedding petals. The men would drink and smoke until they were slurring. Penney would walk Sadie around the block and slip into bed with an airport paperback.

Nothing would happen, except that they would all live until they died.

A *snorf* at the door interrupted her, rude as a blast from an air compressor.

Reese started. She'd not click-latched the door. The investigative snuffs and snorts persisted, pushing, until in the blackness Reese heard the unlatched door give way to the soft jingle of Sadie's metal tag. The jingle marked purposeful rhythm as the big body and vacuuming breath (smell of wet wool and hamburger) trotted toward her own scent, and she waited for the cold wet snout to find her. She leaned down, whispered *Hey*. Sadie nosed Reese's bent neck (it felt like the end of a hose), then snuffed at the immediate bedside. She settled her hindquarters at Reese's feet and mashed her forehead against Reese's knee, aligning her chest and flank to lean along Reese's calves. It was as if the dog were trying to become Reese, or to get inside her and disappear.

The dog parked her velvet throat over Reese's knee, sighing.

Reese couldn't help it: She laughed.

The dog was Buster Keaton.

Then it occurred to Reese that the dog did this each day, with Will.

Pushed her way in. Poked her cold muzzle into Will's hand or lap or behind his knee; fixed him with the fathomless yearning that conferred its instant, inexplicable softening, its chemistry-altering fact. In a way it was like being handed a baby. Will would never cop to it, of course; his manner with the dog was gruff, offhand, even annoyed. But say it or not, Will was getting daily shots of something—unalloyed.

Reese stroked Sadie's warm, smooth head, and her mind's eye roved the rooms of the house, scanning the placement of objects. The coffeepot ready with filter and grounds for next day, the frozen orange juice thawing, the careless mosaic of toothpaste and soap and hairbrush in the bathroom. Plates and books and TV remotes; shoes and telephones; earrings and doormats. Talismans and tokens. Evidence of the living. In a handful of years the stuff would be landfill, or cracked and rusting in shops that smelled like mildew. But for the present the artifacts glowed, numinous expressions of faith. Belief, Reese thought. That thing we do. The punchline of everything. Goldy believed in oblivion, and, dutifully, oblivion came. Assassins and suicide bombers and witch doctors were believers. Belief filled and drove us like wind. Certainly it was hopeless enough on face of it. Here we were all responsible for each other, and somehow we had to keep being that while we watched ourselves fail at it, constantly and grossly. Who could blame anyone for singing *hear us* at the top of his lungs, on the off chance something might be listening?

How brightly, how brightly it shineth.

Come on, girl. Time to sleep.

Reese guided Sadie up by her capacious, white-aproned chest, gently grasped her collar, walked alongside her at a half-crouch through the open bedroom door. For a moment she felt amazed by the giant, docile beast walking quietly with her. She brought the dog into the dark kitchen and squatted there before her, taking the doleful clown-face in both her hands— its smashed-in mug, chalky white-on-black in the darkness, a Rouault portrait. She gave the furry face a gentle shake. Stay, girl. Go to sleep. See you in the morning. In the darkness she could feel the animal's grave attention: lustrous eyes pooling with practiced doubt, an eternal boding mixed with silly hope, for which there was no remedy. There would never be a remedy. The dog folded down onto the linoleum with a resigned, forbearing *snorf,* into her familiar, lonely vigil.